LEGACY

Anna Rashbrook

My thanks to everyone who has supported me with this book.

Dave, as ever for his patience when I spend hours tapping away.

To my friend Hilary, whose support has been a total blessing.

My first readers, Dinnella, Alan, and Lin

ALSO BY ANNA RASHBROOK

Travel Memoirs
Dear Boot
Wish You Were Here - Holiday Memoirs Anthology
The Travel stories Collection (The
Travel Stories Series)

Supernatural Thriller
Tom

WW2 Racing mystery
In Plain Sight

Pit Ponies
Lamplight to Sunlight
Lamplight to Sunlight; Children's edition

Blogs
Blogs 'So Where's the Snow?'

https://annarashbrook.wordpress.com

Anna's Horse Books

https://annarashbrook.wordpress.com

CONTENTS

1 CORINTHIANS CHAPTER 13
New International Version

13 If I speak in the tongues of men or of angels, but do not have love, I am only a resounding gong or a clanging cymbal. 2 If I have the gift of prophecy and can fathom all mysteries and all knowledge, and if I have a faith that can move mountains, but do not have love, I am nothing. 3 If I give all I possess to the poor and give over my body to hardship that I may boast, but do not have love, I gain nothing.

4 Love is patient, love is kind. It does not envy, it does not boast, it is not proud. 5 It does not dishonor others, it is not self-seeking, it is not easily angered, it keeps no record of wrongs. 6 Love does not delight in evil but rejoices with the truth. 7 It always protects, always trusts, always hopes, always perseveres.

8 Love never fails. But where there are prophecies, they will cease; where there are tongues, they will be stilled; where there is knowledge, it will pass away. 9 For we know in part and we prophesy in part, 10 but when completeness comes, what is in part disappears. 11 When I was a child, I talked like a child, I thought like a child, I reasoned like a child. When I became a man, I put the ways of childhood behind me. 12 For now we see only a reflection as in a mirror; then we shall see face to face. Now I know in part; then I shall know fully, even as I am fully known.

13 And now these three remain: faith, hope and love. But the greatest of these is love

IN SPAIN

'I told you that the handbrake was broken.'

Mary and Phil looked down the steep mountain valley to where a plume of smoke made its way up to them from the wreckage of their car. All around, the insects continued their racket as if nothing had happened, and they gloried in the heat of the day. Mary turned, strode from the edge, and sat down against a rock to rummage in the cool box. Inside was soothing chocolate and as she ate, she realised her knees were shaking. She could still hear that crunching on the gravel as the car rolled, rapidly accelerating down the slope to the edge.

'At least we've got plenty of food. Do you want a drink?' She proffered a cake.

Phil pulled himself away from the spectacle and sat beside her without a word. Mary glanced at him and saw he was deep in thought rather than shock. She knew he was best left alone like this, so she swigged her drink and munched his cake.

'We are the dead,' he suddenly quoted from George Orwell. 'All that we had as ourselves is in that car. Passports, laptops, kindles, plane tickets, wallets, cards, and money. Our only possession on earth is that cool box. Do you know, I feel like a weight has lifted from me?'

The awesomeness struck her in another way. 'So how do we get home, or even to the port?

We can't get on the ferry. We can't buy tickets or stay in a hotel. We'll have to go all the way to some city where there's a consulate. We'll need new passports and bank cards. At least I backed up everything last night onto the cloud, so we'll still have the holiday snaps.'

He turned to her with a grin, 'You've missed my point. We're free of our old lives, we can reinvent ourselves as whoever we want.'

'Well, you might have a murky past, but I'm quite happy with me,' she retorted.

'We could start new lives in a new country, away from all my tacky past. No one would be able to find me, I would be free from the shackles.' She saw that smirk through the beard.

He was on about his long-lost daughter again, the one he had spent so much time trying to track down and now he had found her, was running a mile from the commitment of meeting. Pretty much the story of most of his life.

'Think of it,' he continued. 'We've returned the keys to the holiday home and the car rental isn't up for another couple of weeks. That valley down there is devoid of even a manky goat. No one will find that wreck for ages and even then it's so burnt out, they'll think we were in it, any bones eaten by the animals, nicely cooked. And then there'll be an inquest and we'll really be dead.' He was forgetting the tall column of smoke in the windless sky.

'What about my house and all our friends?'

Mary almost choked, seeing grieving relatives at the grave, as well as the complications a sale might bring.

'We agreed that ages ago, as you had no one to leave the house to. Steven is a good solicitor, he can deal with everything. There's my money in the bank account to pay all the direct debits for years. We might come back at any time and say we've been on a world cruise, backpacking and the car thing was all a mistake. We might visit our own memorial, few people can do that.' She imagined his brain running around in all directions, and not getting to the end.

'So now you're going back?' She began to get exasperated.

'No, I have another idea.' He took a deep breath and his bushy eyebrows shot up in the air, a sure sign of some new plan he knew she would need convincing on, like those racing pigeons. 'I suppose you left all the wills and your letters of instructions on the desk like you do in your normal paranoia that we won't get back? Who is it we agreed to be named in the will? Angelika. She'll come to the house when she inherits it and live in it or sell it, but she'll read all about me. See how I lived. She'll know me, and one day, when we return, there won't be all that weeping and snot and soppy stuff.'

Mary hung her head in her hands then burst out laughing, 'If you really think that, you are in la-la land. There would be huge legal recriminations and arguments if we don't do anything and then just turn up.' And you wouldn't be able to stay away from your beloved marshes for long, she voiced to herself.

'Disagree. It will cut the ice, and we can have a great holiday in the meantime.'

That tone of voice was final, so as usual, she went with it.

'And how are we to have a holiday with no money and no ID, we can't even check into a hotel without passports?' she couldn't help asking.

'You know the expression that sailors have a woman in each port? Well, it's still sort of true, but nowadays, also means a bank. I didn't have much time for shopping when I was stuck on all those freighters, so kept it safe. The port of Algeciras Bay isn't far away, and I still have contacts there. Much goes on in those streets behind where the ships dock that is kept quiet. I can soon sort passports, and there's many a lodging house that asks no questions.' Mary saw the slums and red lights above the doors.

'How do you get your money from a bank with a new ID?'

'Well, I might sort of already have it in another name. I was keeping my secret stash for our big anniversary.'

'What if I don't want to die?'

'You'll have a hell of a time explaining my death. Could you carry that off?'

He had her there. She wouldn't be able to

convince anyone of her grief if he was still alive. But a plan of her own was forming at the back of her mind that would thwart his. With any luck, when they signed into a good hotel, there would be a computer and internet. She sighed as he pulled her to her feet, and carrying the cool-box between them, they started their long trek downwards. At least they were both wearing their hiking gear...

A FEW MONTHS LATER

Steven Stephens senior sat at his desk in his quiet little solicitor's office in the seaside town of Bridmouth. He liked a quiet life, and retirement lay a couple of weeks in the future. But now he sat with his head between his hands. What were they up to now? Before him lay a coroner's inquest report, a bill from an irate car hire company, letters from an insurance company, wills and several printed out emails. Not to mention the ones in Spanish he would need translated.

What were they up to now? Were they alive or dead? They were in yet another unholy mess. When would all this stop? The pigeon venture. The grounded, wrecked boat. Going back packing at their time of life. And these were only the daft ideas he knew about. Why didn't they act their age? Why couldn't they just settle down in Eastbourne and be gaga?

Well, this time he was going to fix them for once and for all. Steven Stephens junior would know nothing of all this if they did ever return, and even so, he would make a lot of money from sorting things out. Stiffly, he stood up, grabbed most of the papers, except the wills and coroner's report, and shoved them into the shredder which tore them to unintelligible shreds with glee.

A FEW MONTHS LATER STILL

Early morning sunshine filtered through Angelika's eyelids, closely followed by the sound of cawing seagulls in her ears. She couldn't resist opening her eyes to take in the sights and scenes all around.

The sun had risen, spreading light over the sea, which was in calm mode, with gently rippling waves falling on the beach. A few, happy looking clouds were scudding along. The sand beneath her was warm through her sleeping bag, so she stretched a little and watched some more. A freighter made its slow way along the horizon. Where was it going and what was it carrying? Gold and treasure or car tyres?

A yawn made her think of coffee, so she sat up and rummaged in her backpack for the last in her thermos. Finding a convenient rock behind her, she leant against it and sipped. Perfect start to a pretty important day. And the first day, for what seemed like forever, she was totally alone. She savoured that feeling, but wondered if the thrill would wear off.

The caffeine soon made her restless, so she wriggled out of her bag and packed everything away, leaving nothing behind except the indent of where she had slept. The sandy, stony beach was still devoid of life, except for the seagulls who fought over something on the high tide mark.

Angelika stretched and one of her hands caught in her dreadlocks, it really was time for them to go now that she was a homeowner. She made her way westwards along the beach, hopping over breakwaters, until a curve in the shore made the sea lap against the edge. She clambered up to the top of the grassy bank that ran along the coast into the far distance.

The inland vistas caught her attention. Hamlet couldn't be far away. There had been no sign of a bay where small coastal villages usually clustered on the maps she had looked at, so this bank must run right past it. She sighed in glorious anticipation that all of this would soon be so familiar she wouldn't even notice it, because it was home.

Home! At that moment, one of the clouds covered the sun and it seemed that everything turned cold. She'd left everything because of this inheritance that had arrived in the post, just as she was at a low point in her life. An answer from God, or huge mistake? Shivering slightly, she was glad as the sun returned.

Angelika scanned all around to see how far she had to go. Behind her along the coast were salt marshes which lay on the edge of Bridmouth, the huge seaside town where she had left the train last night. It had taken a long trek to escape the seaside town's bungalows, cafes and promenades, but now they were safely hazy in the far distance. The marshes now merged into farmland with fields of ripening crops, grass, herds of sheep and cattle. Just like a child's toy, the nearest cows all faced in one direction, fiercely munching away.

Beyond them, she saw more trees, and between them some grey tiled rooves. That was it! She strode on, still taking in the new vistas all around her, and soon saw that beyond Hamlet stood green woods, not any nasty regimented pines, but billowing oaks and beeches, and oh, she didn't know their names.

It was all how she had imagined it from her searches on the net, and the little the documents had told her. Now she was going to live in this isolated little part of the world, put down some roots and be still for a while. A glorious sense of freedom and joy filled her, so she thanked God again for his providence.

Soon she saw a track making its way down a field, this must be the road up to the houses. The grassy bank was higher here, and to her surprise, a small house sat tucked down behind it. Must be protected from the wind, she mused. It was long and low, with white walls and all sorts of boaty things lying around. A clanging of rigging on mast caught her attention and, on the sea, a small, moored yacht bobbed on the waves. It must belong to that house, hopefully it wasn't a holiday place.

Within a few yards, a groove on the bank led her way down to the track's level, where she swung through a kissing gate, next to a huge padlocked one, and with rising excitement strode up the gravel track. She jumped as a startled hare ran across her path, or was it a rabbit? She was such a townie and had a lot to learn, but there would be time to do so in her new life.

Her way suddenly swung to the left, and she stood before a huge, very old looking brick and flint building with a roof that dipped slightly in the middle. It must be ancient, Angelika thought, its colours were sort of mixed into the land around.

It was clearly a café of some sort, as picnic benches stood on the patch of grass in front of it. The ground floor windows were almost hidden by huge window boxes of brightly coloured, mismatched flowers. Up in the roof were dormers, and it was capped with a slightly wobbly brick chimney. Angelika stood admiring it, but at the same time feeling sorry that it must be a tourist trap, when the huge front door opened and a woman threw out a bucket of water, narrowly missing the gawping Angelika.

'Oh, good grief, I'm so sorry, there's not usually anyone around so early. Did I soak you?'

'No, you missed, better luck next time.' The pair of them burst into laughter, and in an appraising glance, they took each other in. The woman took in a not so young hippy back packer and inwardly groaned. Angelika saw a woman who wore humour and laughter over hard work and was glad she would live near her as she seemed so solid.

'Would you like a coffee? I'm May and I run this madhouse!' Another grin.

'A strong one would be wonderful.' May beckoned her in, and Angelika followed her up a short flight of steps. She found herself in a dark room filled with a long table with benches and armchairs spread around in total confusion. In one corner was a huge open fire, already filled with logs for winter. Bookcases filled the walls, stuffed with more tomes than in a library. A long counter ran along the back of the room, where May was filling a huge mug.

'Proper coffee this, none of those daft little capsules.'

Angelika warmed to her even more and took the steaming mug. 'Is this a café?'

'Not as you would think it. The coast path runs by here, so we give refreshments to those on the path and the long distance walkers. We also do Airbnb, but we keep it low key, and ask people to give it low ratings, so we know visitors really want to come here. And anyway, we can only cope with so many. Don't want the hordes from Bridmouth finding us.'

'What keeps us going is local people. We sell some honey for Henry up the road and veggies for Mark and Fiona when they have a glut. We have quiz nights and things like that too, but everyone brings their own booze as we don't have a license.

13

That and selling the books online keeps us going nicely. Now, why am I telling you all about this when you're probably just passing through?'

Angelika couldn't not tell this woman who seemed so loving and joyful. 'I'm coming to live here. I've inherited a cottage just up the road and I'm moving in.'

The woman's eyes opened in astonishment, and Angelika saw something like a flash of fear, but perhaps that was the caffeine talking.

'Mary and Phil's place? Are you family? She had no children, and they hadn't been married for long, so I don't know about him.' Her voice was a little gruff.

'No, not family, I hope to find out more later when I meet the solicitor with the keys.'

'We still don't know what happened to them, except they went on holiday last year and never came back. That solicitor was here a while ago and he wouldn't or couldn't tell us more. How exciting for you.' She didn't sound it.

'I'm going to live here, not turn it into a holiday home, if that's what you're thinking.' Angelika gave her what she hoped was a big, confirming grin. That seemed to help, as May, who had gone a little rigid, now relaxed.

'Well, welcome to Hamlet, I know, stupid name, as there is a church, but that's exactly what it is called. There used to be a big house somewhere here, but after the Second world war, both the sons were dead, and the family demolished it to escape death duties. Most of the land was sold off, except this little patch because it's low lying and marshy.'

'Henry Elliot, who farmed here with his son, built a new farmhouse on what we suspect is the site of the house, then the son built yet another on top when Henry retired. We still have the Manor's church and labourers' cottages, oh, you'll soon find out! What time is your appointment?'

'Nine thirty.'

'Well, it's only eight! Why don't you take a walk up to the cattle grid and back then you'll get the lie of the land? You can go through a gate at the side of it. There are thick woods beyond the grid which keeps us out of sight from the main road, but from there it's about a mile to the bus stop. Only a couple of buses a day, but we're always giving each other lifts. Are you bringing a lot of furniture?'

This was an odd question, Angelika felt it slightly nosy.

'Only because it's all as they left it, there's no room for any more, you'll see!' May grinned, as of reading Angelika's mind, but again in that kind way of hers, and Angelika took no more offence. She grinned too, handed over her mug and smiled a farewell.

EXPLORING

The morning had got going in the short time she was inside, warming up all around her. There were clumps of cow parsley on each side of the lane and other plants. She had no idea of their names, but they looked like a colourful old picture. Such greenness after years of city life, was like a gentle balm to her soul. Birds sang everywhere, all it needed was some rustic yokel with a straw in his mouth to give her a nod and some ancient wisdom.

Before long, another house stood on the left, looking much like the café, but smaller, just as old and wrapped into the fields. Angelika surmised they had all been built at the same time when the estate was set up. Did they set up estates? Build or establish?

It was clearly a small holding, as she saw ducks and chickens pottering around in a large paddock. A couple of sheep grazed at the far end with a moth eaten looking cow. Beyond that was a vegetable garden with poles covered in some sort of vine. To Angelika's town based mind, it all looked quite idyllic, although bits of old machinery lay about and peeling bales of something were stacked against a wall.

A door flew open, and a youngish couple, dressed in old clothes and wellies, came bursting out of the front door in full argument, which seemed to be about the cow. Angelika sped up until a tall hedge hid her, hoping they didn't spot her. She didn't want to know what her neighbours were yelling about, it might be embarrassing later when they met up.

As she sped on, there came a small cluster of trees and another brick and flint cottage on her right, hidden from the road. All she could see was a bright orange front door. Was that her new home?

Slowing down after her rush, she now saw that next door was the church. It seemed very small, with a bell tower, and built in the same way as the houses. She passed through the lychgate and all around the graveyard lay a mix of stern Victorian tombs and leaning, moss-covered stones. The long grass hid a smattering of flowers, but there came a sudden sense of peace.

She walked up the steps into the small wooden porch where lay a heap of last year's leaves and a faded sheet of services hanging from a mouldy notice board.

The weathered door opened with the expected creak, but inside was a surprise. All the walls were decorated in a pale blue that gave the whole building an unearthly atmosphere. Plaques to war heroes and people who had done good dotted the walls in stone and badly marked brass.

The pews were old, their contours worn to soft lines by hands rubbing them over the years. A simple altar stood under a clear glass window.

Angelika wondered what had happened to the brightly coloured stained glass, which surely should have been there.

She sat and talked with God, thanking Him yet again for her new home and then simply rested with her hands on her knees, absorbing the atmosphere of the church.

A gust of warm air spiralled through the open door, making her remember her appointment, so she stood up to leave. It was only then that she saw the fresh vase of flowers on the altar, filling the place with their rose like scent. She had come to a good place.

Back on the track, which she now saw was becoming more and more potholed, stood another house on the left, identical to the small holding one, but half was clearly being done up as a mess of builder's gear and material were strewn all over the garden. The other half had a garden full of roses, just coming into bloom, and their scent led Angelika on.

Further on to her right was a long low building, which must have a long time ago been farm workers' cottages because of the repeated front doors. They were clearly filled with families now, with washing waving on a couple of lines, and toys littering the communal gardens, along with bikes and seats. She heard voices talking and sped on, wanting to see this place without having to interact with the people just yet.

There came another long stretch of lane, but

this was lined with an electric fence, the grass clearly munched by cows, and fertilised by them on their way to and from the fields. She smelt their dung and milk as if it clung to the hedge. In one field, several scruffy looking ponies munched on the cropped grass. Angelika guessed there must be some children around to ride them, maybe from the farmworkers' cottages.

Before long, Angelika came two very posh pillars that looked completely out of place. She peered up the muddy drive which ran past a tall green hedge and saw the new farmhouse. No brick here, it was all done up in white pebble dash. A large porch and big generous windows looked towards the sea. Behind it were more brick buildings, clearly the farmyard, where a cow was mooing her heart out.

Angelika's phone beeped with a message, which she ignored, but saw the time. She needed to hurry up if she were to reach the end of the track and get back to meet the solicitor. Well grazed fields were now on either side of her, then came a high wall and another house.

This one must have been older, its roof sagged even more than the others, with windows of tiny, rounded panes. There were even plastered beams like a Tudor house. Some sort of plant grew all over it, and to the front of it was another pond where a couple of white ducks busily dabbled in the water. It had an air of quiet gentility with the flower filled garden surrounding it.

Beyond it, she saw woodland, she must be near the end of the lane. Angelika stood and stared, was this older than the estate? Might it have been a monastery? There were some odd, churchy shaped windows at the end. Whatever it might have been, it was a beautiful house.

A window opened, the panes banging against the walls.

'Get away from here, we don't want your sort here. Go back to your mucky town and stay there!' A walking stick was waved at her. The ranting continued, so she spun around and marched away. The voice stopped as the window slammed.

After a few yards, Angelika heard a rumbling sound, which must be a something crossing the cattle grid. A sleek black car came down the track, setting up a cloud of dust which choked Angelika and got in her eyes. She was fumbling and coughing when she realised the car had stopped and was reversing back. Not another lecture? The window rolled down.

'Miss Smith? I'm so sorry to engulf you, it hasn't rained for weeks. I'm Steven Stephens, I believe we have an appointment. Pop round the side and jump in.'

THE NEW HOME

He didn't say much as they flew down the lane, leaving a cloud behind them, which must have told everyone they of their arrival. They both patted themselves down as they got out of the car. Yes, the mystery cottage was hers, and she followed him through a slightly wonky gate.

He was very quiet as they walked along a brick path bordered with flowers and bushes; it seemed she was going to be a gardener. It led up to that orange front door, which stood up several wooden steps under a large wooden porch, which was filled with coats hung randomly on the walls and piles of boots underneath.

The door opened with a sighing creak, and they entered a hall decorated in shades of green, which made it dark, but light streamed in a window halfway up the stairs in front of them.

Mr Stephens opened the door on the left.

'This is the main room. I'm trying not to sound like an estate agent!' He gave a small smile and Angelika saw he wasn't much older than her, but had thinning black hair and grey eyes. She took herself way from a character assessment and looked around the room.

It was stuffed with comfy well used chairs laden with cushions, every space on the wall was lined with bookcases, and in the corner stood a huge TV. The room felt homely, like the owners would be there in a minute bearing a tray of tea and biscuits. Mr Stephens cleared his throat.

'As I told you, Phil and Mary were on a walking holiday in Spain, when apparently, their car fell over a cliff. The wreck wasn't found for months, and then it took ages for EU officialdom and UK slowness to sort out the estate and track you down.'

'They left you their house and all their assets, which will also take a while to work through probate, but the latest figure looks as though you will come into about £20,000.' Angelika realised he was avoiding eye contact with her and looking towards the window.

'Have you no idea about why they left it all to me?' This was the greatest puzzle and all her searches on the net, records' offices, and ancestry sites had brought no answer.

'None what so ever. I've been through the house as far as possible, there are some letters left on a desk which I have read, as they weren't in an envelope, but they are no more than repeats of the wills and instructions about their things, which I'll have to leave to you to do. There is one major problem, though. There are no deeds. I took over this business from my father, who died recently and unfortunately, a lot of his old files were, for some reason destroyed when he retired. I've been to the land registry, and nothing has been changed since the estate was bought in the 1890s, although there's no legal requirement to do so. Perhaps as you settle in, you will go through all these cupboards and the loft and see if you can find them. Mary's parent's moved in here in the early 1960s, but beyond that, it's all a blank.'

Angelika had been musing a lot about this apparently random gift, and now wondered how he knew about Mary's mother moving in. Then her mind veered off in another direction.

'Is there a chance they will walk back in again?'

'Very unlikely, you should consider this place your own. I'm sorry you've been left with all the contents to deal with. One of Mary's documents said quite explicitly, that it was all to be left as found. Other wise, I would have suggested a house clearance firm came in before you arrived.'

'Did you know them?'

A strange look flitted across his face, but he masked it. 'My father was their solicitor for about five or so years, and, as far as I can find out, most of the business was done over the phone, post and net.'

Angelika had a suspicion he wasn't giving the whole story, but there would be time to dig into it, especially as she got to know the locals. They no doubt would tell her more.

He turned around, almost brushing past her, and went through the door across the hall. This time, he stood aside to let her in and remained silent.

The room was quite different, with wooden floors, more bulging book cases and two desks that sat side by side looking out of sliding doors. The view was of the garden, but faded into significance, for outside was the sea, bound by the grassy sea wall which lay all of about a hundred metres away. Over it she saw the ocean, disappearing into the haze, next stop, America. The two of them stood in silence for a moment.

'This was the dining room, but they put the windows in. Quite something and they're triple glazed against the storms.'

Angelika now looked, one desk was orderly with where a laptop had been, cables, books and files in neat piles. The other looked as if the laptop had been stolen and everything ransacked. She couldn't resist a giggle. 'Definitely a his and hers, who is who?'

'That's for you to sort out.' He sounded uncomfortable. 'Through here is the kitchen, which runs along the back of the house.' He led the way to show her. This was also cosy, but tidy, with a range, wooden table and colourful china on a unit. A door clearly led out into the back garden, and Angelika saw the view was of the fields and woods, a total contrast to the other side and a long garden.

'You have nearly an acre here, there's a chicken run down the end, all the poultry went to the farm, if you want to reclaim them. It's the only farm on this track. Now upstairs.' He strode towards the staircase.

There were three bedrooms, one of which belong clearly to Phil and Mary. Angelika shuddered when she saw the huge double bed covered by a thick quilt. This room looked to the back. A small guestroom which looked towards the chapel was tiny and bare except for the bed. The other bedroom looked to the sea. They stood admiring the view again.

'I guess they couldn't stand the noise from the beach in the winter.' He had read her mind. 'Nice room to sit with a coffee before you start the day.'

Did she hear a touch of envy? It was indeed a lovely room, with double bed, cupboards and a chest of drawers. She would sleep in there regardless of the sea.

The bathroom had a shower over a huge bath, all done in shades of blue. Angelika sighed, for the first time in years, she would have a bathroom to herself, no sharing. As much water as she wanted and as long as she wanted. Bliss.

'There's a loo off the kitchen downstairs.' She turned and saw he was glancing at his watch.

'I've an appointment in an hour. Do you have any questions?' He proffered her a paper file. 'Here are copies of all the documents, and the utility bills I've received. If you have any questions,' he repeated, 'just ring the office, but it's all straightforward. All of the utilities are still connected. They requested that they remained so and had left money in an account for that. Once you have changed all the accounts, contact me and I'll transfer the remaining balance to you.'

He headed towards the stairs, and bounded down them to stand at the front door, rummaging in a pocket. 'Here are the keys to everything, house and all the sheds. I've also left the number of a reliable house clearance firm should you need it.' He proffered his hand, and after a speechless Angelika shook it, he was gone, slamming the door behind him.

ALONE AT LAST

How peculiar. Why had he shown her around, shouldn't he just have handed over the keys? Was it normal or right for a solicitor to go searching through a clients' property? Then why the rush? It was almost as if he had something to hide, but the place was hers.

She was totally overwhelmed. She'd expected a few sticks of furniture to be left and nothing of the people who had lived here. It was an intrusion into their lives, even if they were dead. That made it worse. Feeling ill at ease, she wandered into the kitchen and unconsciously filled the kettle, switched it on and took a mug off a hook. A large jar of coffee stood by the kettle, so she found a spoon in the draining tray and made herself a coffee, she didn't take milk, anyway.

Drawn by the sea views, she walked around and looked out the windows, supping away as coffee was a medicine to cure her ills. She pushed her way between the desks and using the only odd looking key, slid the windows open and stood in the salt laden breeze that wafted into the house.

Besides the briny smell, there came the scent of the garden flowers, grass, and trees. She closed her eyes. This was somewhere, a place she had dreamed of being for many years. She'd smelt this scent at times of stress, sadness, and loneliness. It arrived from somewhere to comfort her and now was real. This must be the place of His safety that he had promised her at those times.

Angelika sank down on the steps, and closer to the earth, prayed. Taken from the Lord's prayer, she had read a series of books where this was known as the ultimate prayer, that never failed. It was short and had so many dimensions.

'Your will be done. Not mine. Your will for my life, which is to prosper me in all ways, to fill me with your spirit, to bring your kingdom on earth. To bring eternal life, health and peace to all.'

She then sat still and prayed in tongues, while seeing in her mind what she had found in the house. His joy and peace filled her, and while she didn't always rely on her emotions, she knew this wasn't of her, and relaxed. This was okay, it was her home, and now she would go back inside and look at the place with calmness and surety.

The kitchen, like in the many houses she had lived in, was the heart of the house and she happily looked in cupboards, and found a well stocked freezer, but an empty fridge, happily cooling nothing. Just as well she never used milk, but she would have to find a shop soon and stock up with the things she liked.

There was a washing machine in the fitted kitchen too, so she cheerfully threw in all the rumpled, dirty clothes from her rucksack and, with two of the capsules from the box on the shelf, set it to work.

Upstairs, she found the airing cupboard, and there was plenty of linen to make up her bed, she almost wished morning had arrived and she was watching the sunrise from her nest of pillows. Bed made, she slung her few toiletries in the bathroom, and looked forward to a long, long soak and read later on. There was no lack of reading matter here, she just hoped there would be something to her taste. You never could tell in someone else's house.

She took her laptop to the tidy desk and respectfully moved everything off it onto the floor. She glimpsed a winking modem and plugged everything in to it. Password? It would mean setting up a new account and that might take days. In annoyance, she switched it off and went into the garden.

It really was a paradise, filled with plants completely unknown to her, but as they were bushes, hopefully they would just need a little looking after. A trodden path led to what must be the hen run, and to her joy, there was a pond. And on it, she was sure, swam the same two white ducks dabbling away. One looked up at her, and she was certain it winked. Her snigger made them take affront and take off to fly towards the sea. Whatever, it felt like a greeting, and she knew they would be back.

The shed was unlocked and inside stood an old freezer filled with feed. Perfect. She'd put some in the hopper by the pond, that would make them stay if she fed them. Angelika didn't fancy having the chickens back, she'd never be able to eat all the eggs, unless you could keep just one or two. She'd have to ask about that.

There was also an over grown vegetable plot, shown by orderly lines of weeds. What plants were edible and which were poisonous was a mystery to her, so she would leave that well alone.

Garden tour over, she returned to the kitchen feeling hungry. She rummaged through the freezer and the well filled shelves. With a microwave ready meal and a bowl of tinned peaches, she dined like a lord at the huge table, raising a glass of wine to Phil and Mary. Better still, when she had searched for plates, she found a small cupboard filled with chocolates and biscuits, so what if their dates were suspect?

Inevitably, she ended back up at her laptop with a sense of frustration. Surely, if these were older people, they might have written their password down somewhere? Much rummaging followed. She didn't really take in what the paper files were at that stage, but they seemed to be stories and essays, Mary had been taking an OU course.

Angelika gave up and sat down to watch TV, another joy to be taken alone, with no battle over the remote, for the first time in many years. The batteries were flat, so that meant another search in the cupboard under the stairs which housed the hoover, and boxes of tools.

On her return, as yes, there had been a box of batteries, she was battling with opening the remote on the table when the coffee mat she rested on shot off and hit the floor.

BINGO! Underneath was written what must only be a password. TV abandoned, she was soon on the net and spent the next couple of hours catching up on emails, her blog and her friends.

Then it was a glorious soak in the bath, powered by an electric boiler with no limit on how much she used, no banging on the door. Afterwards, in her old jamas, she flicked gloriously through the channels until sleep overcame her and she made her way upstairs, to be lulled to sleep in a matter of seconds by the distant sound of the sea.

After a troubled night's sleep, the early morning found Angelika sitting in her bed, looking out of her window, more tired than she had been for years. There had been so many strange sounds in the night that she had woken bewildered. Most of them must be unknown sea birds, one was clearly an owl and then there were strange lights bobbing on the ceiling.

When she heard voices, she thought it was Phil and Mary returning, which terrified her. Then boots scrunched on gravel and she guessed it must be night fishermen. She finally fell into a deep sleep as the sky began to grow light.

What to do now? A day of freedom? She was too used to being busy to relax, read a book and potter all day. In those dim hours she had made a decision, and whether right or wrong, she was going to carry it out; it was as if God had put it in her heart. This was her house, but something connected her to Phil and Mary. She couldn't let them go just yet, but she didn't want to live in this dead peoples' house. Angelika had a lurking worry that she would hear a key in the lock and they would walk in, but maybe this would wear off over time.

She would make a compromise with them. All of their personal objects that were clearly loved, she would box up and move into their bedroom. Then shut the door on it, and perhaps in a year or so, she would be able to make a decision. The furniture was neutral, she would focus on it being like a furnished rental.

It took her all day, the simple things like knick knacks were easy to discern and she swiftly collected ornaments and odd plates from all over the house. All the boots and coats she flung into the empty bedroom cupboard.

The books, she felt, were public domain, so she did no more than cast an eye along the shelves, and found many a book she had read, and others she would like to read, on so many subjects. It was almost like a public library.

Casting her eyes on the walls, she found very few pictures, and these were mostly seascapes that she rather liked. Nowhere, anywhere, were pictures of Mary and Phil. It was as if they had been removed, for there were some un-dusty places on shelves. No photograph albums either. Had Mr Stephens removed them, and why?

The files on the desks proved to be of little interest. Mary, if she returned, might want her OU stuff, and the letters were only instructions on things like the hens and some bills. Phil's papers were printouts of a sailing club, train magazines, nothing personal. Angelika's instinct wondered if the mess had been caused by someone ransacking them. But what proof did she have, anyway, all the personal stuff was most likely on their laptops?

MAY INTRODUCES HERSELF

As she shut the bedroom door firmly on the last load, someone banged on the front door, and Angelika nearly jumped out of her skin, having been so absorbed in the house clearing, she'd lost track of time. As she ran down the stairs, her stomach growled in annoyance.

There, with a big grin on her face, stood May, with an enormous cake in her arms.

'I guessed you might get really busy at settling in, cake always helps!' She almost pushed past Angelika and strode into the kitchen, clearly knowing her way.

'You're having a clear out then? Selling anything?' She looked around quizzically.

'No, I've just moved all the personal stuff into the main bedroom, and I'm shutting the door on it. I feel I'm intruding at the moment, maybe in a few months I'll sort it out.'

'Can understand that. You going to put that kettle on?'

Angelika obeyed, 'I don't have any milk, I'm going to do an online shop later.'

'Don't bother, they won't deliver out here, especially in winter when the potholes are bad. Why don't you drive in?'

'Umm, no car.'

'There's the Land Rover that's up at the farm. They used the posh car when they went away... I guess that's long since been taken in lieu of airport parking fees.'

That was incredible news, although Angelika didn't enjoy driving. 'Can you tell me more about Phil and Mary? There's nothing of them here, it's like all their personal stuff has been taken.'

'Really? There was a picture of them in the hall.' May strode off. 'You're right, perhaps taking it down was in the instructions left for that sneaky solicitor. He came and snooped here quite a lot.'

'He said he was looking for the deeds.'

'Hmm, don't buy that one. He even came to us and asked nosy questions about how long they had been here and their families.'

'Did you tell them?'

'No, but I can tell you. I don't mind my coffee black.'

Angelika took the hint, and cut them large slices of what turned out to be the most wonderful carrot cake.

May began. 'Mary's mum lived here for years, in fact, all the older people were about the same age, there's only Roy's father, Henry left, he's in half the double cottage. He's knocking through, now that twit has gone... I digress. Mary was born here and stayed to look after her mum until she died. She worked in the local supermarket.'

'Never married until about five years ago. Think it was menopause myself, she took herself off on a cruise and returned with Phil. Everyone was suspicious of him at first, but he was a merchant seaman, a fisherman and drank most of us under the table. They were happy together. So he became one of us. But she said he was always having hair brained schemes that she talked him out of, like starting a fishing lake behind the sea bank that's part of your land.'

'You're not going to say that I've a boat, too?' Angelika didn't want a boat at all.

'No, Phil sunk it on one of the sandbanks a few years ago and gave up with it, he wasn't good in a yacht.'

'Did you find out anything about Phil?'

'Nothing except that he'd been in the merchant navy all his life and had travelled the world. We liked them, they were good on quiz nights. Now that reminds me, the next one is the day after tomorrow and we expect you to take their place on the team. Got a speciality?'

'The Bible? You see, I'm a pastor, although I haven't worked in that role for a while.' Angelika saw May stiffen in the way so many people did. 'I've been working with homeless people for several years, and this change has come just at a time when I am completely knackered and worn out.'

The slightly cheeky language seemed to work. 'Well, if you can get people into our little church, you're welcome! We had a sort of minister here many years ago, but he disappeared. There aren't any keys. You can take on the bats!' May really laughed now. 'You're not married then?'

'Nope, gave up on that idea a long time ago, I've been too busy!'

They were now on a second piece of cake and more coffee.

'Were you born anywhere near here?'

Angelika realised it might be easier to tell an official potted story of her life and let that circulate. It would save repeating it every time she met someone, as she had the idea that May would have some sort of network to broadcast it on. Taking a huge bite of cake and washing it down, she gulped and began.

'I was born in Portsmouth, on the rough estate of Paulsgrove.' In her mind she saw her bedroom with the ever dingy quilt, walls that no poster would stick to and the corner that stayed black however much bleach was put on it.

'Our flat was on the ground floor and got all the noise and bother of the street, but my mother revelled in it. There were people in and out all day, drinking or just sitting around nattering, bringing fish and chips to eat if we were lucky. There was often odd smelling tobacco, but she wouldn't allow anything stronger than that, as if she were a saint herself, she would piously say, 'not in front of the kids.'

'It was my normal, and I didn't realise it wasn't until I went to school. I was always on the outside with the other kids from our estate and we were just crowd controlled, not taught.

At secondary it was worse, but Mum did her best to get my uniform, even if it was second hand scruffy.'

'I endured, and after some name calling, began to understand that of all my mother's boyfriends, none of them were my father. When I picked up the courage to ask her, on a day when she was sober, all I got from her was that he'd been a sailor from a passing through container ship. So no hope of escape there.'

'As soon as possible, I stole her money and ran. Luckily for me, it wasn't long before the Salvation Army picked me up, and they sorted me out, although it was hostels, never a home. Got up to all the typical disturbed things a teenager does, managed not to get pregnant, and found Jesus. Studied at Bible school, ran a church for a while, then found a calling for looking after teenagers like myself. Hostel life for twenty years, while I wandered the world in various jobs, which is why I'm so looking forward to some peace here.'

'Aww, you poor duck, but things have come right now.' A suspicious look crossed May's face. 'Not bringing any of those teenagers here?'

'Not likely, this is a whole new start for me. How did you arrive here?

'Married that nutter, my husband, who was born here, and we've had a wonderful life together. Both kids are at university, couldn't be better! Now you get your shopping list written and I'll get Roy from the farm to bring the Land Rover back and you can go shopping.' She bustled out, no doubt to tell everyone the gossip. Angelika grinned to herself and got on with the last few bits of sorting. The house looked bare, no longer Phil and Mary's house, it was a blank canvas.

She strolled out into the garden for some fresh air, and found the two ducks still on the pond, who turned to stare at her. As if trained, she walked to the shed, filled a scoop with grain, and chucked it in the already empty feeder. The two chattered away, or in her made up word, 'chumbled' in their ducky happiness, as they dabbled in the water and stuffed their faces. She had heard their companionable chatter throughout the day, as the windows were wide open. The ducks seemed to sense her every movement and quack. Now she understood they had been asking for food.

SHOPPING

A good night's sleep after binge watching a series on TV had Angelika wondering if she should go and fetch the Land Rover from the farm when she heard an engine and a toot outside. By the time she got her boots on and down the path, the tooter had disappeared and left a note pinned to the windscreen.

Hope you like the old bus! I've filled it up with diesel, and you're covered on the farm insurance until you can get your own cover. Come and have a cuppa with us. Bests, Roy

He must be a busy man, Angelika surmised, crumpling the note up. She swallowed the last piece of carrot cake and fetched her bag. Her shopping list was long, it would take all day to do everything on her list.

She had driven Land Rovers out in Africa, so the jolting, the wobbly steering wheel and the noise of the thing were no problem. What she did have to watch out for were the potholes in the road. By the time she got to the cattle grid at all of twenty mph, she had worked out to follow the zigzag ruts to avoid them.

Angelika had already checked out the shops in Bridmouth online and made her way to one of those which supplied everything for the home and more.

Grabbing a trolley, she entered into a world she had never visited before. Of course she had shopped, but over the years it was always dashing in and out to buy basics, rarely anything for fun. Only sometimes would she lash out on something highly coloured from a market stall. She stood at the door, almost overwhelmed by the colours, scents and bustle. It was only when someone tutted she moved out of the doorway and into the shop.

Childhood had seen hand me downs and tatty scrounged furniture that often had holes with small, itchy visitors. Her time at the Salvation Army had been in hostels which could be made familiar, but never home. Then working a life where she often gave or loaned things meant she never had much, and certainly nothing extravagant. Not even when she was in Bible college for a year.

Angelika entered a world of luxury and wealth as she bought towels, bedding, her own china and cutlery, and daft things like a kitchen radio that looked like a dog, place mats with crazy cows on them, a brightly coloured rug for the sitting room, and deep blue velvet curtains for the living room. The Land Rover filled with carrier bags of joy.

Clothes had been like those her contemporaries wore: hippie, baggy trousers and t-shirts, and loose woolly pullies in winter. She didn't err from this, but found an assistant in one of the pricier shops and together they sorted a new wardrobe suited for country life. It was still garish in colour but new and smelt good. She bought wellies and jackets for all weathers, and best of all, new, pretty underwear.

Then came the big decision. She'd already made an appointment but could easily cancel. The guy with the green hair didn't flinch when she told him what she wanted, and he delivered. He rescued enough of the dreadlocks to give her an elfin haircut with highlights in her brown hair.

She looked back as she left, saw an old friend being swept up, and grinned, it was time to move on. She looked in every available mirror or glossy surface as she shopped in the supermarket, and much of the food was things she'd never eaten before, or had the time or inclination to cook.

It was early evening as she zig zagged back down the gravel track, grinning away and looking at herself in the mirror. And the greatest satisfaction? She hadn't spent a penny of Phil and Mary's money. She wasn't going to touch it if possible. Her hoard had been grown from all her years of work, thrift, and keeping herself safe. Now it was time to enjoy it.

Back in the cottage, she tried all the clothes on. The new underwear felt stiff and would need wearing in, but in hitching her boobs up a bit, it made her stomach flatter. The new trousers and jumpers looked almost too good for her new life. From long experience, she knew how hard she was on her clothes, they would soon be old friends, and she could always buy more. What fun!

Angelika twirled and posed in the long mirror and almost wished she had a friend to call for an opinion. Was she evolving into a new woman after all these years of being part of the scenery? Never mind, the years of changing jobs and travelling meant she had Facebook friends all over the world, she would post pictures on there… no, she wouldn't.

It was nice to have a stocked fridge and looking in it, Angelika suddenly felt guilty after years of living with poor people, those who had little. She was now almost decadent. Am I? She asked God, and sensed only a peace. He knew she was just enjoying something others took for normal. Most of the food she had bought was ready meals, and pre-made stuff, but now she would have toast and cereal, and ice cream when she wanted. And cake, perhaps she would have to learn how to bake, that would be a new goal.

Another box set binge and a whole tub of ice cream had her crawling into bed at some late hour and she woke to the sound of someone again banging on the door. Flinging on her new bright red dressing gown, she thundered down the stairs. May stood there again with a slightly disapproving look on her face.

'Nice lie in then?' She bustled past and sat at

the kitchen table waiting for a cuppa. At least now Angelika could offer her some biscuits and milk for her coffee.

'I was doing a load of shopping, look at these curtains.' They were duly admired.

'When you're putting them up, give me a yell, it's a two man job. At least the old curtain rails are still there. I just popped by to say it's quiz night tonight, and everyone will be there. We won't bite, it's always a laugh. Oh, I've got it now, you've got rid of that manky, matted hair. Suits you!'

'It feels cold, I keep on wanting to put a hat on because my head's so light!'

May sniggered, drained her cup and rose to go. 'You got a specialist subject?'

'The Bible?'

May snorted and trotted off.

REFLECTING

Angelika looked out of the door, and outside was another calm, warm summer day. She really should get some exercise, so she dressed in her new jeans, t-shirt, new bra on the last hole, found her new thick socks and walking boots and took off down the track towards the sea.

On the top of the bank, she looked out to see the clouds playing with a patch of sun on the blue grey water. She was so glad not to have a camera; it was a moment to absorb, not snap and forget the pictures on her phone. The dinging sound of sail on mast caught her attention and saw the yacht slowly making its way towards Bridmouth.

A lone man gave her a wave, but he was in silhouette, so she couldn't make him out. She waved back, everyone must know who she was by now, tonight would probably be a cross between the first day at a new job and meeting long-lost relatives.

Angelika watched the boat disappear into the distance. Who was he? A single man? An old man living out his days? A divorced man suffering from a broken heart? Oh, good grief, she should never have read all those romantic novels a housemate had left behind in the last flat. She was acting like a teenager all over again. She grinned to herself.

Striding along the bank seemed a good idea to rid herself of these daft ideas and she pounded along, listening as her breath got more ragged with the unaccustomed exercise. Enough. She slowed down and saw she was nearly past the woods that protected Hamlet. What lay beyond?

She strode on to find more marshes and another resort in the far distance, but far enough that this path seemed rarely used, there was little rubbish except what seemed to have been washed up.

Angelika jumped down to search for some shells and soon had a small collection that would go on her mantelpiece. That was something she'd never been able to do before, and with it came a sense of something resting on her. She'd never stayed in one place for more than a year, how would she cope with always?

She began to look for blessings. No more long prayer meetings, no more earnest prayers that were really just giving God a list of instructions. No more dealing with other people's problems and life situations that were heartbreaking. No more being moved from job to job. No more difficult workmates. Perhaps now, with quiet reflective times, a serious reading of the Bible, not dictated by a study group's agenda, would be a real thing.

She would renew her mind totally with his word. On her own, there might be a down to it in that there would be no one to bang ideas about with, but then again, she would be able to concentrate on what God wanted to say to her. That was both exciting and daunting. Alone. A whole new world. Prayer walking on the beach, free and open to God.

She sat down by a breakwater and watched the waves and felt hungry. Remembering the mars bar she'd thrown in a pocket, she pulled it out and began to munch, the romantic man coming back into her mind.

Would all this change mean she'd now find a partner? Did she even want one? Had she spent too many years on her own? She thought of her teenage years at school, where the promiscuity she saw in her childhood led her from boy to boy, and into head long crushes that led to heartbreak as they walked away after the first night. She'd been sucked in every time. Yet, the chase and excitement in some ways had suited her. Her grief had been shallow and soon gone when she found a new quarry to hunt.

All too soon, exams came, and they all went their ways, forgetting each other and school in an instant. Angelika ran away from home and never saw any of her friends again. She drew a firm line under that part of her life.

Her new life with the Salvation Army clamped down on her activities, and at work she didn't have time for anything else at the end of the day. Then, when God finally got through to her, she swore off men as she tried to get her life onto some sort of biblical track.

In many ways it was a relief to have the man hunting and the ricocheting from relationship to relationship over. In Bible school, most of the men were either married or so into their faith, they weren't really looking. Yet some of her friends found men with integrity there and married them pretty quickly. At work there were men, but she really couldn't be bothered.

It seemed being in love turned a lot of men into gibbering heaps, and the married ones were the worst. She didn't want any of it, and never stayed in one place or a job long enough to find that man who did it for her. There were fleeting relationships, but they rarely got beyond a few dates before she called time on them. She kept her barriers raised.

This constant travelling over the years had led her to so many different churches and denominations that she refused to be called anything but a Christian who was in a certain type of church at that time.

So what now? Did she want to find someone? Possibly. Would she now find a fellowship where she could settle? Maybe. But the thought of settling down in all the senses felt like a weight in her spirit, so maybe it wasn't God's plan for her just yet. Perhaps she'd simply forget about it all and learn to bake cakes.

DOG

Mars bar gone, she sat enjoying the sea, then had the unnerving sensation that she was being watched. Slowly she turned her head, expecting some other walker, only to see a shaggy brown dog with an even darker brown ear, with his head on one side, giving her a good look over.

'And who are you?'

It took the question as an opportunity to jump down and introduce itself. And check her pockets for any treats.

'Nothing there, mate! Where's your owner?'

The dog sat and looked at her, again with its head over one side, unable to answer. Angelika stood up, jumped up onto the bank and looked both ways. There was no one in sight. The dog jumped up and looked, too.

'Well, you better go and find him. Off you go!' Angelika sort of wafted her hands. It didn't work, so she took off back home, hoping the dog would stop following her. She tried the wafting many times but to no effect, and even shouted, 'blast you, go home!' He followed her right into the café, too.

'Help, May, I'm being followed!'

A short plump, dark haired man looking alarmed stormed out from behind the bar.

'What's going on, do you need help?'

'I'm sorry, that sounded bad, but this dog has followed me all the way back from the beach and I can't shake him off.'

The man relaxed and grinned. 'Hi, I'm Ted, May's husband. Let's have a look.'

He leant down and stroked the dog. 'No collar or ID, I hope she's not been dumped, it's happened before. She looks like a retriever mix, and with that odd ear, she would be easily traceable.'

'Dumped?'

'People from the town let the dogs go in the marshes and disappear. If you go over to the vet's they'll find out if she's chipped. They'll then send her to the RSPCA or some rescue home if not. It's getting late, you'll have to do it in the morning.'

'Can't you keep her for me, I know nothing about dogs?'

'Sorry, we have four out the back. Bring her to the quiz tonight, someone might recognise her.'

It seemed she had little choice, but at least Ted gave her a couple of tins of dog food and Angelika walked home with the dog firmly at her heels. As the door opened, the dog pushed past Angelika as if in a rush to get in, and nearly tripped her up. 'Oh, blast you!' She shouted again in annoyance, but the dog just stopped and looked at her as if in complete ignorance of any wrongdoing.

Angelika made her way to the kitchen and rummaged for bowls. She filled the first with water and the dog greedily splashed and slurped, but quickly lost interest, her attention was on the tins. A complete newbie to dogs, Angelika took the biggest tin, opened it and shoved the whole lot into the bowl.

The dog frantically leapt up and down, and all but jumped into the bowl face first. Angelica watched in horrified amusement as the food disappeared in a matter of seconds. The dog looked up in surprise when the bowl was licked clean, as if asking for more.

'That's your lot, or there'll be nothing for the morning.' To her surprise, the dog almost sighed and then bustled off, clearly to look around the house. The kettle had just boiled when Angelika heard the most awful retching sound. She ran to the sitting room, where the dog had rejected all her food and water, and was now trying to wolf it down again as quickly as possible.

She remembered times when starving children arrived at the centre and must be fed so carefully. Perhaps she should have thought of it, especially if the dog hadn't eaten for days.

'Blast you, nooooo, don't eat it again!'

But the dog had by the time she spoke. At least her new rug looked clean. 'Come on out in the garden before you do that again, come on, now!'

The authority in her voice made the dog follow her, and as they opened the back door, the two ducks sat there, waiting for their feed.

The dog leapt at them, then stopped, looked and sniffed. It was as if something passed between them. The dog sat and looked; the ducks glared back. They soon cheered up when Angelika threw their grain, but it was most odd. Dog and woman walked around the garden for a while, again the vegetables catching her eye, but she had no idea how to begin.

She looked for the first time into the greenhouse and found ripe tomatoes growing from a straggly vine. Treasure indeed. She pocketed a handful and went to make some sandwiches; she didn't know if there would be food at the quiz evening, so this seemed a good idea. The dog followed obediently, seeming to have held on to the regurgitated supper, which Angelika tried not to reflect on.

The dog sat and dribbled while Angelika ate the sandwiches, but she wasn't used to dogs and ignored it. With a couple of hours until going out, she plonked herself on the sofa. Dog followed, and they sat companionably together watching TV until it was time to go.

THE QUIZ NIGHT

It was with a lot of trepidation that Angelika stood outside the door of the café, hearing a babble of voices inside. She mentally braced herself as if going in for an interview, decidedly made a smile and pushed, only, as before, got shoved out of the way by the wretched dog pushing in. At least she didn't stumble over her. A quick yank on the lead soon brought things to order again, and Angelika looked through all these stranger's faces, who would soon be friends, to find May, her port of safety.

Everyone turned to see her, and she was hit by a barrage of greetings, hands held out, and smiling faces.

'Give the woman a chance!' May charged through them all. 'Now, I will do the introductions and then you can all do the small talk through the evening. These two are Roy and Teresa from the farm.' Angelika smiled at a rotund couple; she was dressed smartly, he in t-shirt and jeans with rosy cheeks and could not be anything but a farmer. They grinned back, and Roy winked at her.

Next came his father, Henry, who lived in the cottage that was being done up. He was tall, grey and bespectacled, with heavy horn glasses that made him look slightly like Michael Caine. He had a handshake that nearly broke her hand.

Beside him stood two stretched versions of Roy, his sons, Pete and Ron, standing smiling at her vaguely with their blonde wives, Poppy and Honey at their sides. Both women stepped forward, hugged and air kissed her, then said, come for coffee and natter as if were an order.

Another couple, nearer her age, Mark and Fiona, were the bickering two from the smallholding. They looked tired and worn out, but put on their best smiles. She sensed a tension between them and hoped it was just overwork.

Then a single man, Glen, who seemed the youngest of the lot, tall and broad, with red hair touched with grey. He wore a blue guernsey, so he must be the sailor. He didn't say much, just grinned and sat back down again.

'So that's everyone,' May beamed.

'What about the people at the end house?' Angelika asked. There was a momentary pause.

'Oh, they are quite elderly and don't socialise much. Now tell us about this dog,' asked Henry.

Nicely deflected, thought Angelika. Then came another barrage of talk about the dog and vets and how horrible people were in the towns. A gin and tonic was thrust into her hand, and she was propelled onto a long bench.

'Order, order,' yelled Ted in a good landlord's voice. 'Two teams tonight, just pick a number from the hat and adjust your seating accordingly. No 1 left-hand side of the bench and No 2 on the other.'

There was much thronging, seat swapping and glass hunting. Angelika found herself in the middle, with Henry on one side and Fiona on her left. He leaned to her, 'Any secret knowledge? Good to have someone new with more weapons!'

'Er, Bible and a bit of geography, I've travelled a bit.'

He didn't flinch like May had. 'Marvellous! I'm good on the Second world war and the 1960s, and Fiona is a dab hand with anything to do with plants.'

At the point, Ted got in again. 'Team names?'

'The Secret Weapons,' roared Henry, 'as we've got an unknown quantity!'

'The Management!' came from Roy, 'as we've got the skills.'

After handing out of papers, they were off. It took a couple of hours, a lot of whispering, scratching of heads, and Ron nearly being disqualified for having his phone on, as it rang when it should have been switched off. The Secret Weapons won by two points. There was much cheering and the losing team shared some chocolates they had brought with them.

From then on, it got more boisterous. An old Juke box stood in the corner, and the younger ones got up to dance. Angelika found herself being swung around by Pete, who was quite a dancer for one who spent most of his time in a tractor; that's what she thought he said.

She seemed to have snapshots of people and

conversations during the evening to take home and ponder on. How Ron and Pete, even though one wore a beard, were incredibly alike, as were Poppy and Honey, who wore their hair in identical styles. Henry seemed on another planet at times, suddenly talking about music in the 1960s when on a political question, so she wondered if he was losing the plot, but when they got the answer, his point was linked to it. Angelika was fascinated by that daftness and knew she would enjoy having a coffee with him.

Mark and Fiona were subdued, but she overheard that the previous night they had both been on watch for their late calving cow, only for her to pop the calf as soon as they went in for breakfast.

Roy and Teresa just seemed happy with life and looked with such affection at their children, but did that last when the early rising for milking had them blearily falling out of bed?

It didn't go on late, as Ron and Pete had to be up for the aforesaid early milking. Angelika had been told to come for coffee with everyone, she'd never had such an evening. At the end, she sat with May, Ted, and Glen.

'I must buy you all a nightcap,' Angelika said in a slightly woozy voice.

'Not at all. As I said, we don't have a licence, so we have to buy our own drinks and keep them here. This is your first night, so it was on us. Next month, you should bring a large gin and lots of tonic, or some bottles of wine. Later in the year, we have Teresa's homemade wine to sample,' May grinned.

Angelika realised there were only people from Hamlet there. 'Do you have competitions with pubs around the area?' she asked.

'Not really, we just enjoy our get-togethers. We have our own bonfire night and a Christmas party. And some evenings, we just sort of come down here, all or some. Nothing formal.'

'That sounds lovely. I'll certainly get some drink in for the next evening,' Angelika smiled, but at the same time thinking that it all seemed a little incestuous? No, cliquey. She saw May yawning, so took the hint.

'I'll be off.' She rose, swaying a little. 'Oh, did I come with a dog?'

'She's out the back.' Ted wobbled off behind the bar and yelled, 'Dogs!'

Five dogs of different sizes and colours came flowing out, and proceeded to greet everyone like long-lost friends. Angelika's actually came and sat by her, as if claiming possession, so she patted her head and stood up to leave.

Glen did too, and they left with May, Ted and the pack waving hands and tails by the main door. The fresh air of the night was like perfume and Angelika stood for a moment just savouring it, so different from the stale city smells from her previous life.

'It's special living here.' Glen's deep voice

made her jump, she'd forgotten all about him.

'That looked wonderful when I saw you in your boat. Were you going fishing or something?'

'Just a little cruise down the coast, I've got some lobster pots in one of the bays. Would you like to come out with me one day?' he smiled at her.

'I've never been on a boat before. I might get seasick.'

'You'll have to try it then! Come down next Monday afternoon when the tides are good. Dog can come too.'

He turned to the right, and she thought he waved in the dim light, so she waved in return. Her eyes adjusted to the night, and she made her way back up the path, then jumped out of her skin as a welcome security light came on and she found the front door. It was only then she remembered she'd not locked it, something unthinkable in her old life.

But no work tomorrow, it didn't matter what time she went to bed. She swung up the stairs after locking the door and spent her first night sharing her bed with a dog, who, like most of them, knew how to take up most of it.

VET'S

When Angelika awoke hanging on the edge of her bed, she realised it was her or it. With an almighty shove, she rolled over and, yanking the quilt, tipped the dog onto the floor.

'My bed, and you only come on sufferance. Get it?' She glared at the dog, who sighed and lay down on the floor, as if submitting the point for the moment. Angelika sensed this wasn't the end of the matter, and on reflection, wondered if it was so bad to have a dog on the bed.

'And, anyway, we're going to the vet's straight after breakfast.' She leapt out of bed with her new purpose, then the headache from last night kicked in.

A large glass of water, coffee, paracetamol, and several slices of toast seemed to sort things out. The dog ate her breakfast, didn't return it, and looked for more.

'No way, we're off, they're expecting us.' She grabbed the keys, and the dog followed, unaware that this new home might not be permanent. She jumped eagerly onto the front seat of the Land Rover and sat wagging her tail as they zigzagged up the lane.

The vet's was on the outskirts of Bridmouth, a large, new building, and Angelika heard dogs barking behind it. So did the dog, who crouched down and began to shake. She grabbed her firmly by the collar, which was fortunately not too loose, and dragged the struggling animal in.

The nurse peered over the desk.

'Is this the rescue dog?' she asked in a bored voice and continued after Angelika's nod.

'We will check if the dog has been chipped, and if so, will try to see if the owners' details are on any local or national databases. We will then contact them. If not, we will take a photo and post it on several websites. Then, if there are no results, she will be sent to a re-homing centre.' It sounded like a well-rehearsed spiel.

'How long will this take?'

'Can be up to a month or so, and even if you keep her, the owners may turn up at some stage.'

'Who said I was keeping her?' Angelika said, feeling annoyed.

'If you are surrendering her, then you will have to fill out forms and talk to our manager.'

'Can we try the chip first?'

The nurse came around the desk with a reader and began running it all over the dog, who now became still in fear. There was no beep.

'Could you check the websites?' asked Angelika with a surprising stab of relief.

'I suppose so, she's quite unusually marked, so should come up easily on a search.'

Angelika's mind was in a turmoil as the nurse trotted off. She didn't want a pet, knew nothing about dogs, didn't want the tie. But this was a new life, perhaps it would be ok, her mind seesawed about. She dragged the dog to the chairs. 'Blast you, you're so heavy, now come on!'

'That's an odd name for a dog.'

She hadn't seen the lady with the puppy come in.

'I'm sorry?'

'Stew. She is a meaty sort of brown,' the woman smiled at her.

Angelika got it, she constantly said, 'blast you', in an attempt not to swear. That sealed it, she was keeping Stew. She hugged the dog, who gave her another look. From the treatment room, she heard a male voice singing some song; it triggered a memory, but it was too far away.

Finally, the nurse returned. 'Nothing on the data search.'

'It doesn't matter, I'm keeping her.' Angelika stated firmly.

'That's fine, but I will need to post her details.'

'That's rubbish,' burst out the woman. 'She doesn't have a chip, so the owners have broken the law. She's found the dog; she should keep it.'

The nurse glared, but at that moment Angelika was called in to see the vet. He was tall and tanned with greying hair. When he had finished reading the notes, he looked up and interrupted her musings to agree with the lady outside.

'Another one abandoned in the marshes.

Happens too often. We'll pop a chip in her now, and top up her vaccines, I'll worm her, and give you flea and tick treatment for her. You'll get a reminder next year,' he said. Then glancing towards reception added. 'Yes, she is a touch overzealous!'

'There's one problem. I've never owned a dog before. How much do I feed her? How much exercise?' Angelika faltered, wondering if this really was a good idea.

He looked up from where he was checking a still shaking Stew's teeth. 'She's not very old, and just let me check something.' He expertly flipped the dog over onto her back before she retaliated and looked at her stomach. 'She's been spayed, so she will run to fat if she doesn't have enough exercise. I'll weigh her for the medication, then I'll give you some leaflets to take with you. Do you have any friends with dogs? They are sure to help.'

Angelika nodded, thinking of May and Ted. Half an hour later, she was back in the Land Rover with a delighted Stew. The back seat was strewn with feed bowls, a cuddly dog bed, bags of food and samples to try, leaflets galore, and Angelika considerably poorer. Stew wore a new, properly fitting collar, with a disc to be engraved with a phone number. The nurse had got her revenge.

VISITORS

'So you think it's not such a bad thing having a dog on the bed' Angelika asked. She and Stew were sitting on one of the benches out side the café, enjoying some morning sun with May and Ted.

'Well, with one it's not so bad, but with four there isn't much room. We have a mattress on the floor for them now,' Ted grinned.

'And you might need to keep a window open if they've eaten something ripe,' May laughed. 'We wouldn't be without them, would we, dear?'

Ted did a mock grimace. 'And as for the lead and recall, someone has done you a favour as she's wonderfully obedient.' He had just been testing Stew's paces out on the grass. 'But do keep treats in your pocket as a reward and never be cross when she returns if she's naughty, they can soon learn that it's not fun to come back.'

Angelika absorbed this wisdom as Ted let the other dogs out and they exercised themselves while their owners sat.

'Can't sit here all morning,' Ted finally said. 'That wood for the burner won't cut itself, and you're supposed to be going shopping. My order has arrived at the plumbers and I need it to fix that loo this afternoon.'

Angelika smiled to herself as she saw another side to May as she got up to do his bidding without any argument. Calling Stew, who came eventually, not wanting to leave her new friends, they made their goodbyes and went for a walk through the fields. Everyone could use them, so long as they picked up the poop. She wasn't quite so keen on this bit of dog ownership.

Later that afternoon, Angelika was sitting in the garden enjoying some more sunshine when a click at the gate sent Stew rushing off, barking at the top of her voice. Mark and Fiona were approaching slowly up the path, looking closely at all her plants.

'I'm no gardener, I've no idea what to do here. I expect to your expert eyes it's a disaster!' Angelika thought she'd get that in quick as she went to greet them. Stew rushed around with a stick in her mouth, they stooped to pat her and she trotted off quietly.

'We'd never dare to say that!' laughed Mark. 'Phil and Mary were such keen gardeners we used to bow down to their prowess.'

'Phew, I've got a hard act to follow then.' Angelika laughed, but inside groaned.

'Oh, please don't think we've come to inspect!' There was a plaintive tone in Fiona's voice.

'I'm going to give you the guided tour anyway, as I need to sort out things that even I can see need cutting back.'

Angelika led them around what she called in her mind, the grounds, showing them the ducks on the pond, who were trying to have a nap on the bank, but forced themselves to swim over in case they brought some bread. Then they swam off in a huff, as there wasn't any.

Mark and Fiona didn't say much apart from muttering names of the plants, buddleia, hydrangea, clematis, and nodding knowledgably until in desperation to stop them, she took them into the kitchen for a drink.

'We must come clean, we came and cut some things back last autumn. There is a mower in the shed, I can show you how to use that,' began Mark.

'A ride on one?' Angelika had always fancied burning around on one of those.

'Yes, it is.'

'Oh mega! Now what do I do about what was the vegetable plot?' This had been troubling her for a while, she hated things going to waste.

'Do you want to grow stuff?' They peered closely at her.

'Well, not really. It just seems the thing to do.'

'Then don't. We have a proposition for you.'

'Go on, I'm all ears!'

'As you know, we grow veggies and fruit and have a few of our own livestock. Living the Good Life, you might say,' Mark started.

Angelika read the tiredness in their eyes again. 'And you would love some help?'

'You said the other evening you had a lot of time on your hands.' Fiona twisted awkwardly on her chair.

'Correct, and it wasn't just the gin talking… go on.'

'Would you have the time to come over on a Thursday and help us either with picking, sorting and packing or with the animals?'

She was good at reacting swiftly to snap decisions from her work and also, because something leapt a little inside her as she asked God, with the best prayer in the world, 'Help.'

Fiona had an almost pleading tone in her voice. 'It would only be during the busiest summer months, later, after the potatoes are done, the cabbages and root crops can be dug during the week, they don't need to be so fresh,'

'Hey, it's ok, don't worry. Yes, I'll give it a go, but you know I have absolutely no experience. I've worked all my life with children and on mission.' They didn't pick up on the missionary bit like many people did. Not wanting to or ignoring it?

'It's not rocket science, you'll soon pick it up.' Mark echoed Fiona's grin of relief. There was a hint of relieved tears on her face, too.

'You do realise you might have taken on a duffer, don't you?' Angelika tried to lighten the situation.

'And of course, we'll pay you in veggies and give you a hand with the garden. If you mow the vegetable plot like we said, it will look after itself too.' Mark continued, ignoring her remark.

'Now, that's talking, might there be some milk? When I lived in New Zealand, we had it fresh in our coffees, that was amazing. I looked at your house the other day, is it the same age as the café?' Angelika's mind went off at one of its tangents.

'Yes, most of the houses were built at the

same time as the big house.'

Angelika looked at Mark.

'I guess you know it was knocked down just after the end of the Second world war. No sons to take over and heavy death duties. No one's quite sure where it lay. Our place, we think, belonged to the estate manager, and the head gardener as it's larger than the others. We knocked it through.'

'Did you move from the town when you bought it?' She was on a Good Life tack again.

'No, I inherited it from my parents,' Fiona smiled. 'It was a wonderful place for us kids to grow up in. Now we really must be getting back. We'll see you officially next Thursday then, if not before?'

Fiona's smile seemed a little fixed. What had she said wrong? Ooh, maybe there were dark secrets? Angelika's nosy self was intrigued. The two scuttled off, surely to stop the conversation. Most interesting. She waved them goodbye at the gate and had a go at starting the mower herself.

THE CHAPEL

The following morning began with bright sunlight streaming through the bedroom windows, Angelika threw back her quilt and felt stiff throughout her body. Grass cutting hadn't been a problem, it had been raking up the piles of cuttings, heaving them into the trailer and shoving them onto the compost heap at the back of the garden that had caused it. Was she cut out to be a gardener? Perhaps she was simply unfit. A new life, new things, never too late for a change. Stew barked and ran to the bedroom door, ready for her breakfast.

Over the ever needed coffee, Angelika let the dog out and idly looked at the calendar. It was Sunday. As a Christian, she knew she rested in the peace of God all the time, but it was still good to have one day put aside from everything else. She would go up to the little chapel, tidy up and clean, then sit, pray and possibly God would send someone to share the morning with her.

Stew seemed quite content being left alone with an enormous hide chew. So, with a happy heart, knowing she wouldn't be wondering what the dog was up to, Angelika gathered brushes, mop, cloths and buckets and made her short way up the lane.

The door creaked open, and the smell of damp mixed with old wood leaked out. She wedged a bucket to keep the door wide open and swept the porch free of all the detritus the wind had blown in. Pulling the old service sheet off the door, she found it so bleached that she would never find which diocese it was under. That set her free, if no one had been here for so long, they wouldn't be popping around today.

It didn't take long to sweep out the pews, around the altar and aisle. As the cloud of dust flew out of the porch, she realised she was doing the job twice. There was a pile of dusty blue hymnbooks. The browning pages fell out like leaves, so she dumped them in her bin bag. Polishing the pews with wax and cloth soon had them glowing again.

When she got to the altar, she found fresh flowers again in the small vase and looked around in surprise, in case she had missed someone. The chapel was silent and empty, no one else there.

Reverently, she took the vase and put it on the side, then pulled the mildewy altar cloth off. Behind the altar, she found another old, embroidered cloth in a box, with daisies and greenery all around the edges. Once on the altar, it brought a little light in and the vase of flowers sent colourful dapples onto the white.

Now all it needed for was a rub with Brasso to bring a shine to the old family plaques and window cleaner for the thoroughly grimy glass. The lack of colourful stained glass would mean the light would stream in when she had cleaned it. There was no vestry door or even a vestry, which was unusual. Perhaps the vicar had lived in her house and just walked over?

That was enough. She bundled all the cleaning stuff together, swept all the last bits out into the graveyard and dumped the tools in the porch. Taking her Bible, she sat in the pew and read her favourite piece, the beginning of the Gospel of John.

In the beginning was the Word, and the Word was with God, and the Word was God. He was with God in the beginning. Through him all things were made; without him nothing was made that has been made. In him was life, and that life was the light of all mankind. The light shines in the darkness, and the darkness has not overcome it.

This mystic gospel always blew her away, that something so hippie like had been written before they had even existed. These verses had appealed to many of the often way out people she worked with and had been a bridge between them.

As the words spoke to her, she became aware of someone quietly entering the door. She didn't move, but respected that quiet entrance. The person sat on the pew behind and she heard some quiet words being said. After a while came a voice, somewhat nasal, husky, and slowly spoken with a hint of a lisp.

'I hope you like my flowers.'

Angelika turned, and having had a clue in the speech, didn't pause, but broke into a smile.

'They are absolutely beautiful. Do you pick them yourself?'

'Yes. I have my own garden and I have lots of flowers in it. Would you like to see it one day?' The voice remained slow and husky despite clearly being happy, as a wide grin was now on her face.

'I'm Angelika and I've just come to live here.' She proffered her hand, the woman stood up and came to shake it.

'I'm Lady Dulcie Margaret Hutton and I live with my mother in our home.' Angelika took in the greying, thin hair, high forehead, sunken, slanted eyes, and with a smile replied, 'I live next door to the church. Do you come here every Sunday?'

She nodded.

'Do you like to sing in church too?' Angelika asked.

A wistful look came across her face, 'Oh yes, I miss it so much since they stopped having that funny man here, it's been too quiet for so long.'

'You mean the vicar?

'Yes, his name was Gerard.'

'What shall we sing?'

Dulcie burst into Shine Jesus Shine and the two of them belted it out together, full of joy. They then progressed into three more songs, but then they were out of steam. Angelika heard that Dulcie's voice was deep and mellow, unlike her own slightly shrill tones.

71

'I enjoyed that!' Dulcie said in her calm, if breathless voice. 'But I have to go now, Mother is waiting for us to have lunch.'

Angelika was engulfed in a huge, strong hug. Despite her bulk Dulcie, went as silently as the breeze. It was only as she walked away that Angelika could see her ill fitting clothes and wonder about her story.

Phew, what an answer to a prayer which left so many questions gambolling around her head. The professional saw Down's syndrome and assessed her as high functioning which was something to rejoice in. The nosy part was asking questions. Where did Dulcie live? What was her home like? What was her mother like? All of those questions would be answered when God decided it would be the right time. Whatever, it had been a real blessing.

Back at the house, after throwing some bits into a bag for a picnic, she and Stew walked along the coast beyond where they had met. The dog jumped in and out of the sea and Angelika paddled too. They got to the beginning of the next seaside resort, then walked home to a microwave supper and another night with the TV.

This new companionship grew on Angelika each day, the affection, the movement keeping things alive in the house. She discovered the joy of a dog snuggling up, with no other agenda than wanting to be with her, and no complicated conversations. She just wished her bed was larger, as Stew was adept at getting most of it. It led her to wonder, that where Stew was such a loving, well-adjusted dog, how could someone have ever let her go?

SAILING

Monday was the big day. Angelika couldn't help but be nervous, she'd never been on a boat in her life, ferries yes, but they were hardly the same thing, were they? In the morning, she popped into the café to have a quick chat with May and tell her all her news. Stew rushed straight out the back to see her friends, forgetting about her owner.

It was dark going in, but once her eyes were accustomed, she saw May searching frantically through the shelves.

'Morning love, bit of a panic here. We've got an order for a rare book we've listed, but I can't find it. The Light on the Meadow, by an obscure writer who's suddenly got popular. It's without a dust jacket, dark blue and quite slim. Can you start at that end and check again for me?'

What else could she do? It was such a frustrating search too, as she wanted to stop and browse through so many of the books, whether old or new. So she prayed, Lord, where is it? A dark corner caught her attention and there, sat by a book leaking pages so it was almost hidden, she found it.

'Bingo!' Angelika liked that word.

'Oh, that's amazing! What was it you were saying just before?' May grinned her relief.

'I asked God to help me!'

May shot her a really odd look, but said nothing as she began turning the pages of the book to check it's condition.

'I can't understand the fascination with this writer, but I've had an offer of £150 for this. That will help the kitty. I'll just give it to Ted, who can contact the buyer. Now, come and tell us about your weekend.'

She bustled off and returned with mugs of coffee and the obligatory cake, this time chocolate, heaving under a burden of thick icing. 'We were rushed off our feet yesterday afternoon, its high season and so many people are on the coast path and divert in for a cuppa. I don't suppose you could come on Sunday afternoons and help serve?'

'But of course, I worked in a café for years,' was Angelika's usual impulsive reply, but again, deep down it felt ok.

'We can't pay you much.'

'Don't worry, perhaps you would pay me with the occasional book? I've seen several written by my favourite author here. I've never been anywhere long enough to make my own bookshelf, although I might have to bring some of the books from the house to make room.'

'Deal, we all win.' May sliced the cake.

'I visited the little chapel and gave it a clean yesterday,' said Angelika.

'No one's been there since the last minister passed on. The church lost interest in our little

Hamlet years ago,' but she didn't sound that aggrieved.

'I met a woman there, she said her name was Dulcie.'

At that, May froze, and turned pale, her cake halfway to her mouth. Angelika almost sensed the cogs whirling inside May's head as she put the cake down. She looked quite ashen.

'Don't get too involved with that lot from the house at the end, as we've said. They've caused trouble for us over the years and we keep well away.'

'What a shame, she struck me as lonely.'

'That's as may be, her mother is the worst, really Angelika, don't get involved, they're poison.'

Angelika was so shocked at this that she dropped her cake into her cup. May broke out in almost hysterical laughter. 'Good grief, I didn't mean to upset you. It's just they're not neighbourly and can be interfering. Let me get you another cup and you go and a browse for a book or two.'

May trotted off, and when she returned, they quickly re-found their usual bonhomie, but the neighbours weren't mentioned again.

Later that day, Angelika's ears rang with so many instructions and tips from May and Ted abut sailing as she trotted down the track to Glen's house that her head got everything confused. Perhaps it would be better to just let him tell her all she needed.

His house looked even more picturesque as

she got closer. All the pieces of driftwood, buoys, oyster crates were piled almost artistically along the whitewashed walls. Like the old pictures too, there was a bench and table facing the sea in the sunshine, ready for cups of tea and chats. It was all quiet, with only the sea lapping on the other side of the bank. Had he forgotten?

'Perfect timing!' Glen jumped down over the bank, landing at her side, almost scaring her into orbit. 'Gosh, I thought you'd heard me coming down. No dog?' he grinned.

'She's quite happy at home. I wanted to have this experience all to myself!' Angelika grinned, having returned to the ground. 'And yes, I'm rather inclined to jump at things.'

'I'm afraid the weather is against us, there is no wind at all, dead calm. We'll use the motor and I'll tell you about the sailing bit.' He reached for her hand and lugged her up the bank. The boat was moored right next to it, as the tide was high. He jumped on, and while the boat still rocked, reached again to her, grabbed her hand again, and she found herself on board. He pointed to some seats at the back, so she sat down and looked around her.

To be so close to the sea, and be above it and yet in it, was a revelation. A whole new world. Glen cast off, then he sat with her and he started the motor with a waft of diesel smoke. The motor roared, so at first their conversation was shouted.

'We're just going to pootle down the coast to the other side of Bridmouth, have a spot of tea, then sail back if the wind has picked up. What do you think?'

'Perfect, I don't know how long I should leave the dog in house, would we be back by six?'

'Easily, quicker if we get a breeze.'

There seemed to be a lull in conversation with the noise, so she took the time to study the sea. It really was an almost glassy blue, as all the books said, with odd pieces of weed, wood, and plastic floating past. Sometimes with the light the sea looked green, but she couldn't see far down like in a lake.

She imagined the seabed far below, the fish, shipwrecks and mermaids. Of storms and a ship with a captain who slept through the thunder and lightning. She trailed her hands through the waves, which were choppier than by the beach, until two slapping together slapped her in the face too, with a cold, salty smack. She jumped and saw Glen laughing at her.

'It does that sometimes! Not far now, look towards the coast, we're just passing Bridmouth.'

She looked, and it was a revelation to see a familiar place from the angle of the sea. Being lower, bobbing up and down, made familiar landmarks look small and people on the beach tiny. The big wheel looked out of context, too large. She smelt the fish and chips, heard the roundabouts, and the shrieks of those in the sea, or was she just imagining it?

All she saw was on the horizon, so all the

hotels and roads vanished beyond it, making it like a flat screen. The town disappeared and the suburban sprawl lessened along the coast, and she saw an inlet in the marshes. They turned and chugged up a small river. Before long, they approached a wooden pier, the engine shut down, and Glen threw a rope around a bollard. Once again, his hand was on hers and she was lugged up a ladder onto the pier.

'Thank you for letting me enjoy that, I've never been on the sea before,' she smiled at him.

'I saw you were immersed in it; we'll make a sailor of you yet. The pub's just down here.'

They followed a river path and came to a thatched house, with tables and chairs set around it, filled with people drinking and enjoying the afternoon. There were noisy drinkers and families with children running amok around a small playground. It was almost like a reverse of the café at Hamlet, far more commercialised. She began to understand how wise May was to keep the crowds at bay by writing bad reviews. They soon found a table in the shade and Glen ordered two teas.

'It's better here off season, but it's not too bad today, is it?' Glen asked.

'No, there's not too many people! I can see it could get packed. I suppose most people come by road?'

'Yes, but isn't it more romantic by the sea?'

Slightly startled at that, she grinned nevertheless.

Two strangers, they were both a bit tongue tied on what to say.

'Have you lived in the cottage for long?' Angelika finally managed.

'A couple of years. It's been in the family for ages. I can work from home here as surprisingly the internet is fast in Hamlet, so I quit the city job and set up on my own doing people's websites and sorting problems out. I go up to town if needed, but after all those years in London, it's still like being on permanent holiday.'

'I can see that, in the short time I've been here, I've sensed a relaxing feeling all around me and people are so friendly. So many of them have roped me into helping with things like the market garden and in the café, so I won't get bored.'

'Did you leave a job when you inherited the place?'

Surely the grapevine should have filled him in on all that?

'I'd been working on mission abroad, and was job hunting without much success and, so it was a Godsend, in a way.'

'Mission as in the church?'

Did she see that look that came so often?

'Yes, I'm also a pastor, but I've not run a parish for a long time.' She wasn't going to add that she had lost her spiritual anointing for the work a while ago. The joy and fulfilment that her ministry had given her had disappeared, leaving a dis-satisfaction. So she had left her last ministry to find out what God had in stall for her.

'Dog collar and all? You didn't appear the type when you arrived with all those dreadlocks. We all thought the new look was an improvement! We had a vicar in the family once, it all came to a messy end.'

They burst out laughing, and as their cream teas arrived, the ice was broken. They chatted about work and life, but he didn't open up about his private life so she didn't about hers. He began talking about his passion for sailing and as she was new to it all, what might have become boring became interesting. She bombarded him with questions about the sea, the races he'd done and even some of the basics of how to do it.

'Look, the tide's dropping, we need to go to catch it if we want to use the breeze, it's picked up enough to raise the sail,' he suddenly said, looking out to sea.

The sail back wasn't such an idyll as she learnt how to pull ropes, watch the sail, and duck for jibes, but it was fun. The tide had dropped a lot back at Hamlet, so they moored in shallow water and paddled back with their trousers rolled up, which ended up in a splashing session. Soaked, they clambered up the bank and looked at the small settlement of houses.

'Do you know anything about the family at the end? May was very adamant that I should steer clear of them,' Angelika just had to ask.

'Not really, I just go up to the café for

books and socialising,' came the typical male uninterested in gossip answer. 'Would you like to come in for a beer?'

'No, I've left Stew for too long, she might have eaten the furniture!'

'I'm away next week,' he pulled a face, 'how about some more sailing practice when I'm back? Stew can come too and wear a life jacket and be safe so we could go out all day.'

'That would be fab, I think I might get hooked on sailing!'

'Aha, so I've converted the converted!' he sniggered, 'see you soon!'

Angelika waved and made her way home, wondering how much May had seen and what would be the gossip tonight. As she walked, she heard in the distance a strong, strangely familiar tenor voice singing something she vaguely recognised, but not when or where she had heard it before. It faded on the breeze before she could remember it. The sea had enchanted her, and she really looked forward to more sailing; it was understandable how people got hooked on it. Then it struck her that Glen was the only one so far who hadn't wanted her to do something for them but had given. Most interesting.

A LOST DUCK AND
HELPING OUT

Stew's greeting was the most effusive that Angelika had ever received in her life. For someone to be so delighted to greet her, bowled her over. She sat down, hugged the wriggling dog, and rewarded her with another chew. No furniture had been destroyed, there was only a large dimple in the softest cushion on the sofa. The two snuggled down to eat and watch TV.

It seemed that summer would never fade, and the next morning there were no clouds and Angelika wondered what to do with her day. A swim? Tackle the mess in the big bedroom? Sort out the books? Take Stew for another long walk? Go shopping? The world was her oyster. Peering out of the kitchen window, she saw only one duck swimming around on the pond. It was the drake, and he looked sad, as if a duck could.

An investigation by Angelika and Stew found no trace of his wife. She decided that the best action was to go and ask at the farm. Perhaps she should have shut the ducks in, maybe a fox had got the duck. Her heart sunk.

Mistress and dog met Roy following the cows back out to the field after milking. He looked as if he were born to his job and full of joy in it, as he walked along in his dungarees, cap on head and hand in pockets. All he needed was a bit of grass to chew, she thought. The cows, with empty udders swinging, were keen to get munching, and filed away in a brisk manner. She waited until he had put the electric fence across and explained.

'Could be a fox, they can strike at any time of the year. But it's odd that one is left. Those two have been hanging around here since spring. Best you pop in the house and ask Poppy as she looks after all our poultry, they're all in this morning, so expect a welcome. I must be away to the feed suppliers.'

The two cottages were identical, and she didn't know who lived in which one, so she banged on the nearest wooden door. Both gardens were still strewn with toys in various stages of breakage, amidst chairs and tables.

There was a cacophony of barking and two Labradors barged out as Poppy, or was it Honey, opened the door. Stew was more than delighted to meet new friends, and they all tore around the garden.

'Oh, hi, ignore the dogs, and come and have a coffee.' Angelika followed her into a tidy, clean, and very modern house, which was a total surprise after the chaos of the garden.

'The kids are out riding, so we can chat.'

Angelika slid onto a shiny stool at a breakfast bar as the coffee machine burbled away. Poppy or Honey, who at this early hour was smartly dressed and made up, much to her surprise, banged on the wall.

'Poppy will be round; she's probably feeding the baby,' Honey smiled.

So now she knew at least which was which. The coffee thankfully came in a chunky mug and Angelika explained about the ducks. To her shock, Honey burst out laughing.

'Can tell you're new to farming. They're a pair, she'll have a nice little nest somewhere where you can't find it. Give it a couple of weeks, and she'll march out from nowhere with a clutch of ducklings!'

Angelika could have died from embarrassment.

'Don't worry, when I first met Pete, I called their bull a heifer, he didn't let me forget it for weeks. How are you settling in? Not lonely down there?'

'I'm really enjoying not having to work and getting to know my new home. I went sailing with Glen yesterday.' Oops, wrong thing to say, as Honey cackled with laughter.

'He's a bit of ok, isn't he? One of the strong but silent types. You never married?'

No holding back here then.

'No, never got around to it, my job has had me travelling around the world,' Angelika evaded.

'That must have been fun, furthest we've got away was a weekend in Paris. He's married to this farm, but I knew what I was getting into.'

Just then, Poppy bundled in with a small struggling person under her arms. She released the child onto the floor for him or her to make a beeline for a toy box, which he started to empty.

'It never stays tidy long,' sighed Honey.

'How many children have you got?' Angelika was fascinated.

'Both got three at different ages. In case no one's told you, we're twins too,' said Honey.

'I did have an idea,' Angelika grinned.

'I've got Ann, who is ten, Paul eight, and Tina seven, just don't ask about how that age gap happened. Poppy's got Kevin, eleven, Simon, nine, and that one, the monster Clive, two,' grinned Honey. Angelika's head began to spin, she'd never remember all those names, it was worse than running a kids' club at church.

Time flew as the girls, as she could only see them, told her all about their kids, life on the farm, asked her whether she'd like any more ducks, which Angelika carefully replied, 'not at the moment.' Then they took her to see all the hens, including those which had lived with Phil and Mary. They just didn't appeal like ducks, and she was happy to leave them there.

Then the other five children turned up on the collection of motley ponies. She stroked the hairy noses and explained she'd never had anything to do with horses, and no, she didn't want to try today. The children took off to turn to ponies out. Angelika collected an exhausted Stew who was playing with Poppy's dogs too and began making her good byes.

Then, just as she had expected, they asked, 'I don't suppose you'd babysit for us sometime, the in-laws keep going on holidays and there's no one?' What could she do but agree? At least there weren't any small babies.

As dog and mistress walked along the track, a voice came over the hedge, 'Cooee, come and have a bit of respite after that lot, the kettle's on.'

It was Teresa, who continued. 'Roy's gone off to market and I could do with some company.' Angelika followed the hedge to a gate and went through it to the most amazing garden. She stood and looked, it made her place feel like a jumble sale. Here stood herbaceous borders, rose bed, and shrubs of every colour and size. It was like something from a catalogue or a showplace on Gardeners' world, which Angelika had seen an episode of.

'Isn't it beautiful?' Teresa joined her, 'when Roy's father, Henry, took over the farm, only this patch was left behind, all grown over and muddy. When Henry moved out all those years ago, and we moved in, it became my passion as the boys grew up and I had time on my hands.'

'It's stunning,' Angelika smiled. 'It makes my little garden look drab.'

'Phil and Mary and I were keen gardeners together, we used to swap cuttings and plants,' she said wistfully. 'But never mind, one of the grandchildren is showing an interest, so not all is lost. Coffee?'

Angelika felt overloaded with caffeine. 'Some water? I've had several coffees with Honey and Poppy.'

'Lovely girls, aren't they? We're so happy for the boys. They wouldn't move in here, but that set up with them next door to each other works really well. They had a double wedding too.'

Angelika followed Teresa's tightly permed blonde hair and smart outfit into the house. She couldn't imagine her ever getting behind the wheel of a tractor or mucking out.

The house was cool after the warmth of the day, and they entered into a working kitchen with a huge table and every sort of cooking appliance imaginable, Teresa must love to cook, too. She poured some home made elderflower syrup into tall glasses and topped up with tap water. It was wonderful.

'Do sit down!' They settled on a couple of stools, with an exhausted Stew dozing under the table. There were no dogs or cats here, which Angelika thought odd in a farmhouse. 'We built this from the old farmhouse that Henry built, it was in such a state, he'd done a rush job so he had a home. We couldn't do what we wanted with it, so we re-designed. All the old farm buildings are still around the back.'

Why was she telling her this?

'We rattle around a bit in this house, but

I'm sure one of the grandchildren or more will take it over. Henry built his farmhouse from what he found, there was demolition stuff all over the place. We never did find a map with the original, demolished house on it. The family was what you might say, eccentric. The last relatives live in the old house at the top of the road, and they're really quite odd, don't get too involved in them, they can turn on you in a second and it can get nasty.'

So she was the one they had elected to warn her off. Wasn't going to happen, and she wouldn't cause trouble for Dulcie, either.

'I know about them, but I'm rarely up that part of Hamlet, so I guess it won't be an issue.' Phew, hopefully that would do the trick.

Teresa smiled as if an onerous task was done. 'Do have a bottle of this cordial to take home. I can't believe how fast the summer is flying past, I guess it's the lovely weather. Now, I've a question, do you like blackberries? I like to make jam for everyone, but picking them is getting difficult. I've a touch of arthritis in my hands, do you think you might help me in gathering them? The grandchildren are keen, but they eat more than they harvest and then squash them, and it isn't really the girls' thing.'

Angelika envisaged the long nails coming off on bushes and grinned. 'I'd love to, are there sloes, I'd like to make some gin?' She always enjoyed foraging for wild food, and on some of her trips abroad had learnt how to make a meal from the most unlikely sources.

'Yes, there's so much here for free, there's elderberries, damsons too, and we've a huge orchard if you want some apples. I've been trying to get the boys to make a press so we can make cider and juice.' Teresa grinned broadly at Angelika, seeming so pleased to find someone who might be interested in these things.

They chatted some more, and now the ice had been broken, Angelika sensed a loneliness in Teresa that matched something in herself. Was it a mother figure thing? Whatever, it was the beginning of a friendship that she felt would be treasured by them both... even if again she had been asked to do something.

Soon after, Angelika made her way back down the track, clutching her bottle of juice. She had just got to Henry's cottages and was thinking of food when there came a hiss from behind the hedge. Stew barked and rustled through it, so Angelika walked back to the gate where she found Henry sat on the ground, groping around for his glasses.

'Thank heavens, it's you. If it had been the family, I would be in for a lecture. I came out to check if the builders were here, forgot my phone and slipped on some tarpaulins they left behind. Rotten lot they are, if I could I'd be doing this knocking through myself, I would. Give us a hand up, dear.'

Angelika, having worked in hospitals and

with drunks, swiftly helped him up and gave him his specs.

'You've done that before!'

'I certainly have.'

Henry, once up, seemed in command again. 'Come and see what they're doing.' He led the way. Angelika, now seeing him for the first time in daylight, realised he was much older than she thought. He must be in his eighties at least, with his bent back, thinness and deep-set eyes.

'I'm making two more en-suite bedrooms upstairs, and extending my kitchen on the ground floor, but putting some of these bi-fold doors on the end so I can sit and watch the sea.'

As they turned around the heap of building stuff, she saw why. Although further from the sea, he had an unhindered view all the way along the coast.

'Oh, that is stunning. What a place to watch the sea at any time of the year.'

'My exact sentiments, you will be the first to come and sit with me to watch for the green flash at sunset. Maybe one of the great grand kids will have this place when I'm gone. I'm seeing it as a family home, but for now, it will be my palace,' he grinned down at her. 'Would you and your hound like a spot of lunch? I see you've already been to the farmhouse.'

'I must admit to being peckish after such a long morning, so yes, please.'

Angelika followed him into the other part of

the house, and as he walked, she saw the frailty that had made him fall. In the kitchen, which was delightfully untidy after the other houses, he swept the newspaper off the table and simply placed bread, cheese, pickle and plates before them and they tucked into wedge like sandwiches. Stew helped with the offcuts.

'That's filled a gap,' he grinned. 'I get Teresa delivering me food that I find indigestible at times, so any excuse to go back to basics. Ann, my beloved wife, was an amazing cook. I can still smell her cottage pie.' His eyes went dreamy.

'Teresa told me you built the original farmhouse.'

'I did indeed, I well remember those crazy, wonderful days.' His eyes turned dreamy again, as he was clearly remembering some good times, then he pulled back to the subject. 'It was hard work back in the sixties when I got the place and built my little farmhouse from debris left around Hamlet,' he gave a huge gusty laugh.

'I love building almost more than farming. We made a go of it, and Roy and the boys are taking it further. I'm so proud. They've even got their hands on some of the land I couldn't, and that herd wins prizes at all the shows. Not so sure about these alpacas they're talking about. They grew a field of echium last year, it was a glorious colour and the bees made the most incredible honey too. Made a huge profit, it's used for something those idiot vegans eat. Trouble was, it did self seed a bit, I guess that was all gone over before you arrived.'

'You keep bees? That's something I've always been fascinated with, could I see them?'

He leapt up in enthusiasm and they spent an hour or so looking at the hives, discussing bees, and what she would need to learn and do. He was pleased that she showed no fear, remarking the bees would read that in her.

By the time Angelika and Stew got back home that afternoon, they both had been sworn to secrecy about the fall and had swapped phone numbers with Henry. They were socialised out, glad to shut the door and not talk for a while.

The drake still swam in a bored manner on the pond, so she fed him and as she turned back to the house, his mate appeared from somewhere near the shed.

All was well, and so she christened them Mr and Mrs in readiness for the arrival of the ducklings.

THE TIME IN BETWEEN

The months flowed into each other as the hot summer slipped into an idyllic, cooler version of itself, and finally into a brown autumn. It was a time of growth, settling and maturing for Angelika as she echoed the seasons in her new life. All those requests for help had been a way into the community, and they let her in as she moved into their lives.

Her need to serve people was met, and she felt like it was being said to her, that the biggest way of showing them God's love was how she was with them, so she did all with a joyful, loving heart that prayed for them too. She let God guide her, ready for when the time came to talk freely to them about him and his love. Her Bible became filled with notes as understanding leapt off the pages to her as never before.

Her new friendships in Hamlet were totally engrossing, so with that, her internet friends and acquaintances dwindled, as well as her contacts from work. It was like a door shutting on all those years, and while they had been good, she had no regrets apart from one. She knew her time as a pastor was over, and while she missed the joy of looking after a flock, this knowledge stopped her in her tracks when she wanted to do full on ministry. God was quite clear on that.

Her worry about being alone was groundless. There was a new balance in her life, she could pick and choose when to be alone and when to be with people, something that had never been her decision before. They weren't work colleagues either; they became a sort of fledgling family, if this was what a family was like. Everyone let her into their lives, but not in too deep, which suited her fine.

She made the house more and more of herself, trading many books with May, until lots of the shelves were filled with her choices. Any ones she found with worn, dog-eared pages, she put on a case in the hall for the memory of Phil and Mary. She had no sense of their presence anymore; they had vanished, there were no hauntings or restless spirits. She prayed in the house and sensed its peace enveloping her as she settled into this new life. Everyone took her at face value as she did them and she felt she was getting to know herself as never in the past.

Someone new was emerging from the old Angelika, a better, new person. Having her own space and privacy meant she was rested and slept as never before. Like the morning when Mark had banged on her door at 5 a.m, asking her to help with an unexpected order. She leapt out of bed to help without a second thought. No bad temper, she had willingly helped, like another time when Poppy had all the kids down with a bug, she stayed overnight and let her have a night's rest. No problem was too big.

During a wet spell, she made it up into the attic, which was a huge disappointment.

Despite the solicitor's hints, there was nothing to rummage in, only a box of Christmas decorations and some old coats. All that she saw was that it had been well insulated and nothing more. She shut the hatch firmly on it until Advent.

Angelika emailed Steven to say that she couldn't find the deeds, but there was no response, so perhaps he had lost interest now the estate was sorted out. She had a lot of money sitting in her bank account, which she steadfastly tried to ignore. It didn't rub well with her, and she knew one day she would have to take responsibility for it.

She continued her secret services with Dulcie, who, despite talking about her mother being on her tail all the time, she never came to collect Dulcie, or cause trouble. They prayed and sang, which improved when Angelika took her CD player in and they had some accompaniment, and they weren't so aware of their voices.

Their prayers together were simply for Dulcie's mother, who seemed to tell her off for a lot of things, whether she was guilty or not. Dulcie had an awareness of the world around her from TV, so they prayed for the world and all the crises, and that some more people would join them. That didn't happen, most walkers and passers-by stayed near the coast and rarely came up the lane. Despite that, church was good, and Angelika was peaceful to let things amble along like this.

She missed Glen, who had been away far longer than he'd said. The rumours on pub quiz nights were that he'd either fallen in love, got a new job, or he'd just got bored with the simple life. Angelika was sad, for that fleeting friendship had been a good one, and perhaps there was some life in it. Often she picked up her phone to drop him a message about something she'd seen on the sea or another one of the daft things Stew did, but her courage failed her. She didn't want to spoil whatever had begun by being pushy as she saw herself in the past.

The quiz nights, now that she was an accepted part of the community, were fun and often riotous. On one occasion, they visited a pub on the outskirts of Bridmouth, and had firmly beaten everyone and so far hadn't been back. May for some reason hadn't wanted to offer a return bout.

Waiting at table on a Sunday at May's cafe returned Angelika to her teenage. She'd quite forgotten about how her feet would ache by the time they all trotted off into the sunset, and just how bolshie and stupid some people could be. She was more than glad when the visitors decreased as the schools returned after the holidays. And of course, rummaging in the laden bookcases was always a joy. Angelika found again many books she had read in childhood, and returning to them as the evenings closed in was a joy.

As was gardening. When she went to Mark and Fiona's place, she had been astonished at the amount of land they worked that wasn't visible from the road. So many lines of so many vegetables, some of which she couldn't name, nor ever tasted. She soon learned how harvesting was backbreaking, with the pulling out of the ground by hand, trimming, then placing in boxes.

Her hands cracked as the soil leached the oil out of her skin, but she soon discovered rubber gloves and industrial strength hand cream. For the first few weeks, she was exhausted by it after the one day, and couldn't see how they did it all the time. Then her muscles learnt the rhythms, and it became easier. She knew she'd never be a gardener, even though she perceived the joy and achievement in the harvest of crops that had been sown, cared for and even fought for when the conditions were bad or insects attacked.

Fiona and Mark let her into their lives as she won their respect for her work. They were childless, only mentioning that once, she sensed it was a closed subject because they had been through so much. All she could do for them in this new friendship was to pray for their peace and healing and that it wasn't too late for a baby. Yes, they argued, as she had heard on the first day, but they worked through it. The cow had been an impulse buy by Fiona and Mark felt it didn't pay its way, even though he enjoyed the milk.

The smallholding kept them going, along with the long, hot holidays they would take when there were gaps in the crops. When they told her about these, Angelika groaned inside that she might be expected to come and care for the animals, but to her relief, it seemed Roy and his sons did that. Yet, like all the others, although they hadn't met them themselves, Mark and Fiona echoed every now and then the warning to stay clear of the house at the end.

Teresa hadn't directly mentioned it again, and they spent some wonderful afternoons out in the field, coming home with hands stained with fruit juice, and sometimes their faces were, too. Angelika learnt about making jam, bottling fruit and even making some wine, which when ready came with a warning not to drink too much at once.

While they picked, they talked about everything under the sun, finding a chattiness between them that meant they never were lost for something to say. It was the first time she'd had an older woman as a friend. Angelika wondered if there might be a danger of casting her as a mother figure, especially as nothing seemed off limits in their wide-ranging conversations. These times were a great treasure to Angelika, and she hoped they were for Teresa as well.

Angelika was even invited to the harvest festival meal they held in the house. She suggested the church, but they weren't keen, it was a family thing. They celebrated with a side of ham and a huge joint of beef with trimmings, followed by an enormous crumble filled with fruits gathered from the hedges. Angelika had never been in a large family before and it took her breath away when she realised all she had missed in her own childhood. She decided God was giving her a gift in this and enjoyed every minute, even if she returned home with a bloated stomach and a headache.

It was somewhat like that when she babysat the children too, but here she had training. All the children piled into one of the houses. There was a connecting door she hadn't seen, so that made it easier when some went go to bed. She organised noisy games, then when things relaxed, put on DVDs, and often, even the oldest ones were asleep in their own beds when the parents returned.

The children offered her rides on the ponies as a thank you, but she dodged that. She did enjoy the extra eggs that she received as payment and even baked some cakes with them, but they never reached the tastiness of May's ones.

Henry, she only rescued once more, and on warm evenings, he showed her how to work with the bees and gave her books on their lore, ready for her own hive when they woke in the spring.

Mr and Mrs were the proud parents of six bonnie ducklings, who were a constant source of delight and amusement, and each one ate as much grain, if not more, than their parents. They showed no sign of moving on from the pond, so Angelika, with help from either Ron or Pete, she wasn't sure, moved a hen house nearer the pond to make them a winter home.

And Stew? She wasn't claimed and Angelika basked in that wonderful relationship between dog and owner, an appreciation society which needed only two members, even if one hogged the bed. Stew's friendly, unconditional presence made life more than just a little happy. For once in her lifetime, Angelika was staying put, not getting itchy feet for something new when her life became mundane or boring.

Towards the end of sunny October came rumours that Glen's yacht had been seen moored in Bridmouth, which made Angelika's spirit leap. There was a definite change in the air.

HENRY'S BIRTHDAY

Everyone had been commanded by his Royal Highness to attend his birthday party, which would be in the café so that everyone would fit in, although his house was pretty well finished. There were strict orders for no presents, just plenty of alcohol and cake.

Of course, no one took any notice of that for an 80th birthday, so there had been much discussion on what to give. In the end, there had been a whip around and a palace of a new beehive had been ordered and hidden for several weeks in the shed behind the café.

It was a most wonderful day for November, unusually warm, and very still. The children even went in for a swim but didn't last long in the water as it had already lost much of its summer warmth. In the late afternoon, as Angelika walked along the sea bank, she saw Glen waving to her and pointing to the bench outside the cottage.

'Come and have a beer, it's like summer again, isn't it?' he called.

The glistening bottle was cool in her hand and she sank down beside him. Stew, still soaking from her dip in the sea, lay down for a rest under the bench.

There was something different about Glen, then she got it, his hair was dark brown. He caught her glance.

'I know, hideous, isn't it? After we had our trip, I went to London and then flew to the USA on a big promotional job for a new company. I had to do a video, and for some reason, they took a great exception to my ginger hair and made me do this. And they made me wear makeup,' he sounded totally disgusted. 'I'm not going to get caught on that again. If there's a next time, I'll send a stooge.'

'I quite like ginger hair. You can clip the brown off once you have some of your own colour through again.' Something echoed in the back of Angelika's mind, someone she had known a long time ago; a distant memory?

'That's an idea. Look, I'm sorry we never made our sailing trip, and now I've laid the boat up for the winter in Bridmouth, but what about next spring if you're still going to be here?'

'I've no plans, I'm settling in and getting to know everyone. There's such a family feeling here.'

He looked at her sideways, 'I suppose so, but they can be slightly cliquey too.'

His remark unnerved her, as she had never seen Hamlet in that light, 'I can see that now you say it, but I'm still a newcomer. Have you given for Henry's beehive?'

'May arrived before I had unpacked!' They grinned and clinked their bottles together, 'cheers.'

Angelika revelled in the simply being with him in the moment, and crushed that temptation of asking him if he had missed her. From nowhere, came a gust of wind that was so sharp and cold, they almost dropped their drinks. It disappeared as fast as it arrived. They looked at each other in puzzlement.

'More odd weather, it might snow tomorrow!' Glen laughed.

'There's nothing on the horizon, except a small cloud in the distance,' Angelika looked along the coast.

'Quite often get a blow this time of the year, that's why my boat's all safe and sound. I take it you're partying tonight?' asked Glen.

'Like I could miss it!' Angelika laughed and glanced at her watch. 'I must away and get changed. Thanks for the beer, see you later!'

She returned his bottle and set off home, trying not to look back at him, and not really understanding why she wanted to, either. Half way along the track, she was hit with another squall of cold air that nearly knocked her off her feet and Stew actually fell down on her side. Then it blew away and equally quickly, the warmth returned.

Bewildered, Angelika walked on, wondering if this was something that would happen each time there was odd weather. Looking back at the sea, the now menacing cloud towered over the bank; it seemed to have tripled in size since she had first seen it. This sent a shiver down her back, and Stew seemed as equally pleased when they got to the house by charging in first.

Later on, the pair went to feed the ducks,

but couldn't find them, even when they looked in the henhouse, which was their favourite place at night. Looking up, Angelika saw many V's of birds flying overhead, along with others in groups. She'd never seen so many birds on the move, it was incredible they all migrated at the same time like this; she hadn't known gulls migrated, did they?

Worried about the ducks, she returned to the house, and, as she shut the door, another squall sent the windows rattling. Stew was already on her bed. Perhaps there would be a storm, so Angelika checked round and made sure all the windows were firmly shut and especially the big garden ones had their shutters fixed in place. She'd experienced some terrific storms in Africa, so she couldn't see that a coastal one would be a problem.

Later that afternoon, as she left the house, it was ominously dark for the time of day, and that cloud filled the entire sky. Dark and threatening, it seemed to her that it was an odd colour too, with even greens and pinks flashing through the edges. The wind picked up and was a constant, not gusting, and the air was much cooler. The oddest thing was that her ears ached and popped, something that hadn't happened since school when she had been prone to ear infections. Could it be a bug from one of the kids? She'd been babysitting earlier in the week.

There were several vehicles parked outside the café, which was unusual, maybe they didn't want a soaking when they all trooped home later that night. Hopefully, May might lend her an umbrella if it poured down, but it wasn't far. The door slammed behind her in the wind and she found the café full up; she was the last to arrive, and she lived the nearest.

'About time too!' Glen came over and took her coat, he was ever the gentleman. 'We're all stuffing our faces with pizza, come quickly before it gets cold.' They piled onto the seats with the others at the long table and Angelika raised her glass to Henry, who sat regally at the end, he returned the toast with a huge grin.

The conversation was loud, especially with the children being manic with excitement. After the pizza was cleared away, there was a pause as everyone waited for the cake to be brought in. In that lull, they all became aware that the wind had risen and there was a continuous roar. Outside was now pitch black, far too early in the evening.

Henry broke the moment of worry. 'Another flipping storm, where's my cake?'

May and Ted tottered in with a gigantic, iced beehive and even Henry was momentarily silenced. 'Well, I never,' he said in a louder than normal voice to drown the roar. 'I hope it is actually a cake?'

Everyone laughed and Roy came round with a cooker lighter and lit the candles, which brightened even the furthest corner of the room. What could top that, but everyone singing Happy Birthday at the top of their voices and then having to help him blow the candles? It seemed dark when they were out. The cake was rapidly cut and enormous slices handed around. Someone put the music on in the corner, loud 1960s hits of Henry's era, and he sang, ate, and slurped his wine.

Roy and Teresa then called attention by banging on the table with a hammer. In the hush, the roar seemed even louder and one of the little ones started crying. In came the two eldest boys with the new beehive, and Henry's glass stopped halfway up. For once he was stumped for words and got to his feet to lift the roof and inspect the inside.

'I said no pressies, but this is astounding. Totally, utterly perfect. I will present this to my best colony in the morning. Although saying that, they were rather grumpy this afternoon and for the first time in years, I was stung.'

'Had you been on the gin already?' laughed Roy and everyone joined in. From then, the music was louder, and the children started dancing to the music that they knew so well because it was always on in Henry's house.

Angelika found herself getting steadily intoxicated and was pulled to dance with Ron, or was it Pete?

THE LEGACY

From outside came the most almighty crash, which drowned the music and at the same time, the lights went out. A cloud of smoke, dust, and rain came pouring out of the fireplace, drenching the fire. In the darkness, the children began screaming and Honey and Poppy gathered them to the table to keep them away from the mess.

May grabbed the candle lighter and, in what seemed like seconds, lit the ornamental candles that were standing around the room. As she finished, the men came in from the kitchen area with oil hurricane lamps. Soon it was nearly as bright as before and the children were pacified while they still clung to their mothers. Everyone else just looked at each other, then as one went to the door. Angelika saw they were wrestling it open, and when they did, the wind and rain roared in, sending anything light flying around the room when the door was shoved shut after Roy struggled out.

May, Angelika and the mums put their utmost into reassuring the children, with songs and stories, and they gradually calmed. Then with a bang, the room went flying and Roy burst in. He shouted the news over the chaos.

'The chimney has blown down, and the wind is getting higher by the minute. It's heaving with rain and I heard the sea coming over the bank. The waves are incredibly high,' he shouted. 'There's water coming up the track, so we need to move the cows and ponies up to the higher ground through the woods.'

'Nigel and Fiona, get your cow, and we'll drive it and the herd up through the fields. Henry, you stay here with all the girls and kids. The storm isn't at its worst yet and it's a spring tide at midnight, I'll need as much help as possible. The phone lines are down, but we will be back as soon as we can, don't move.' Everyone piled out of the door as fast as they could, leaving May, Henry, Teresa, and Angelika with the children.

'I'll take them into the kitchen and they can have some warm milk, the aga won't go out as its coal,' Teresa ordered, but in a kind voice, forgetting it wasn't her own house. 'Angelika, you stay here with Henry, he's at the rambling stage, but it's warm enough in here. I don't want him telling the kids ghost stories and starting them off again. Honey and Poppy, bring some wine with you.'

The room emptied, leaving the two of them with the roar of the storm, which seemed even louder. They could now pick out the rain, which sounded like it was sand blasting the windows. Stew escaped from the kitchen and jumped onto Angelika's lap, nearly knocking her off the seat.

'Faithful little hound,' smiled Henry, 'I miss my last one, but the walks would just be too much for me.' Angelika realised he was talking at the top of his voice and she had trouble getting all he said. He pointed to the corner seat, so they took some cake and wine and sat in the snug corner, where, with walls on two sides, it was a little better.

'I've been wanting to talk to you about some things for a long time, but they all piled in on me, forbidding me to say a word, because they didn't want you drawn into it all. Now fill up my glass again and I'll get this told before they all come back, if I don't lose my voice!'

'The sixties were a wonderful time to be growing up in, and the decades that came after it didn't have the freshness and excitement that we had. I'm sure you've read enough books and seen TV stuff about them, so I'm going to take it you get it, ok?'

Angelika nodded.

'I arrived in London, fresh from Yorkshire, having escaped the family farm to start a new life and career in something shining and wonderful. But the rooms I found and the job as a builder's mate didn't quite meet that dream. Then one Saturday night I found the Dustbin Club. It was called that because it was in an old warehouse just behind the local municipal waste depot.'

'It had all the cliches, the wine bottles with candles stuck in them to dribble down the side, the glass coffee cups, and the alcohol. There was a dancefloor made from old sleepers and the stage where groups would come and play on Saturday nights hoping a talent spotter would find them and they would rise to glory. And it did happen, Brian Poole and the Tremeloes played several times there, and after we left. I digress.'

'I went there with some mates from work, but they said it wasn't loud enough for them and they went on elsewhere. I found myself at one of those tables, tapping my feet and loving the music, and there probably was something extra in my cigarettes. Before long, I was joined by a gang of new people. We were very formal and did introductions, then we raved about the bands and the club. I even found myself on the dancefloor, I could shift in those days, you know.'

'It became like that every weekend, and I lived for my time there. We formed a close-knit group of about twenty-five, if that sounds possible to you. We would party too, and even hang out in people's squats. Sometimes it was nearly impossible to get up on Monday, but I needed the money to fund all this. We all worked and there was this excitement for this new life, so unlike our families and homes.'

'Then Veronica and some friends turned up. She was beautiful, charismatic, tall, slender and, oh, so funny. She and her friends were well heeled public school kids, and it was easy to latch on to their money for drinks and stuff. They sort of led the way, and some more of the lads dropped out and we didn't see them again. The drugs got stronger and more expensive, too. Then one bank holiday, we went to Veronica's place in the country for a weekend long party. There was talk that the Hollies might play, so we were off, piling into a train carriage and annoying everyone so much, we nearly got thrown off.'

'Once off the train, we walked flipping miles along the coast to get there, but there was a lot of skinny dipping and fun on the way. We walked up this track to a beautiful house with a pond, and partied like there was another war coming and we had to use everything up.'

He was quiet for a moment, travelling back to that time, and Angelika had a sneaking suspicion about which house he was talking about.

Henry gathered himself into the present. 'When Tuesday came, no one made a move to return to London, and Veronica got up, totally naked on the table and said she was staying. It was her house and we were all welcome to come and live in her commune.'

'So I stayed, I suppose in my befuddled state I thought she would pay for everything. For a while it was a blast, but even her money ran out, so we started growing our own food, and some found jobs. A hazy, happy time, and we shared everything, and I mean everything,' he gave her the nod, expecting her to understand. The wind roared some more.

'Then we noticed that Veronica was putting on weight, and she proudly announced she was having everyone's baby. She tried to cut down on things, but it was all around, it would have tried a saint to keep off it. One night, we were all sitting around when she stood up and gave us a speech about what she wanted to do. She rambled about how her real home had been knocked down after the war. This was all that was left and, as she was now twenty-one, it was hers. She produced a notepad and began writing. We watched in the usual haze until she handed each sheet out. She gave us all the houses here in Hamlet.'

'I'm the only one left now, I was the youngest in the group, but I was given the farmland, as they called me farmer boy, so I had to build my own house. Over the next couple of weeks, we all stumbled off and found our inheritances, and a few even moved in, although there were no facilities like electric or water. But at the weekend we'd all be partying at Veronica's.'

'So everyone here is the child or grandchild of that group? Angelika liked to get things straight. Henry nodded.

'We were proud of our commune and felt we were at the leading edge of something new and there was even talk of getting one of the papers to do an article on us.'

There was another tremendous crash somewhere in the distance, but neither took much notice.

'Then came the night when the baby was born. A girl with dark hair like her mother, she named her Dulcie.'

Now Angelika really gasped.

'But there was something wrong, and Veronica started to bleed, and we could do nothing to help her and she faded before our eyes. She died. For once, we all had to sober up and you bet we did. None of us wanted to lose our new homes, so the next night, we sneaked down to the graveyard, buried her, and put the grass back as quickly as possible to make sure no attention was raised. There wasn't a vicar at the time, so we all felt fairly sure we would get away with it.'

'One of the girls, Heather, said she would care for Dulcie, I think she was one of those who didn't get a house present, so we were all quite happy for her to do so. She was much younger than most of us, she'd drifted in at a party one weekend and stayed.'

'The trouble was a lot of the group left, and before long, she and the baby were alone in the house. Our great commune had failed. So we supported her and the baby. Between us, we paid the bills and got her food. It seemed there was no family left, so no one came to check up and the years began to rush past as we all grew up, settled, and had families of our own. Except for that idiot Gerard who lived next door to me, he grew pot for years instead of a family. The bees didn't like the smell of it, so once he died, I burnt all that I found in his house. That wasn't a good idea as the bees and I were stoned, and of course, Roy came and gave me a telling off. A couple of years ago, I found the piece of paper that Veronica had given Gerard, so I claimed ownership of his house.'

'So how many illicit burials are in the

graveyard?'

'Veronica and Gerard, he had no relatives. Others were dealt with by families,' Henry said matter of factly.

'Now you must hear the end of it. As Dulcie grew, it was clear she was Mongoloid – I know I'm not supposed to say that, but that's how it was. We realised she wouldn't be going to a school, so we paid for tutors and extra help. They became a very close couple, but Heather has never told her that she wasn't Dulcie's real mother.'

'Now, over the past couple of years, things have changed. Heather has become, well, difficult with her demands and has withdrawn. They had always led a quiet life, and it suited us all. But it's coming to the stage that Heather has to be helped, or put in a home, she's become almost violent at times. Trouble is that there would be no one to look after Dulcie. We've just let things slide, and when you turned up, we decided to keep you in the dark, because there's more issues.'

'Dulcie's birth has never been recorded. There would be all sorts of ratifications if it came to light, as well as how the houses were given out all those years ago. No one has dared to trace any of Veronica's relatives in case they came and took the houses away. Of course, if we have to bury Heather, as far as people know, she's Veronica. What if family turned up, like you, for example? We've become what the commune wanted to be in the first place, a community caring for itself. But for all the wrong reasons. It was easier to keep things quiet and let them slide,' he repeated.

The two sat for a moment and listened to the roar of the wind.

'I can look after Dulcie.'

Henry either didn't hear her, or ignored her offer.

'And if we put Heather in a home, heaven knows what she might tell, or even if we had outside help. It's an impasse, and it's easiest to leave the pair as they are. How could we even trust you, a stranger, with all this? You are one of us, and although I've been brow beaten over this, I want it all to end, but I'm as worried as the rest of them.'

And there the conversation ended as the front door was thrown open and several figures, now clad in waterproofs and sou'westers fell indoors, all talking at once. The children rushed out of the kitchen at the voices and were reunited with their fathers.

Roy took command when the hubbub died down.

'It's got worse. The sea bank has been breached. The water from the high tide is flooding in and the rain is torrential, even if the wind is beginning to abate, it may come back again. We've moved the cows and the ponies, so all the animals are safe, but the state of our houses will have to wait until the morning. Is there any chance of something to drink?'

What followed was the longest night in

Angelika's life, no one except the children slept well. All the adults waited for daylight to reveal what the damage was. Henry didn't reveal to anyone else that he had spilled the beans, so for the moment Angelika felt it was best left to slide, she was as bad as the rest of them.

In the early hours, the wind picked up again for a while and then blew itself out, but that didn't calm the waves or the rain or the flood. It was at that point too that Angelika's tired and still drunken brain made a connection, had no one checked on Heather and Dulcie?

THE MORNING AFTER

Everyone must have dosed off, as Angelika found herself wide awake amongst snores and snuffles. Stew snuggled up to her, but that seemed little comfort, she wanted Glen's strong, comforting presence. All that Henry had told her galloped around in her head. How could a lie be perpetrated for so long, that it had become a deep, festering secret?

It shocked her how what had begun as good will had been corrupted over the decades. All that Dulcie must have missed out on in life. How Heather's life must have been so restricted by the secret. Was it this that has sent her potty? What about her family, did they think Heather lost or dead? Did Angelika want to be part of a community that lived on a lie that possibly a good solicitor could sort out, after all, they all had their letters signed by Veronica?

Was it now some sort of ingrained resentment? Had their hate and fear of the pair got out of hand, so they hadn't even checked up on them in the storm? Her head was in a total spin. She'd never been part of a group of people who were so far from God and, she felt completely unable to cope with the revelation.

It was getting light at last, the wind really had dropped, so she went to a window and rubbed a little of the condensation away. What she saw was incredible. Between the café and the sea lay nothing except water. She couldn't see how deep it was, except it that was everywhere. Where the bank had been breached, she saw down to the furious sea, still throwing waves on the beach which flowed through the gap.

Her worry for the two women rose, how could she get out of the cafe? Any movement would disturb someone or a dog. Could she swim there? Certainly the Land Rover would make it, but a tractor might be better. There was one parked outside, but she'd never driven one. However, it gave her an idea of the depth of the water; it was only halfway up the wheels, so about two or three feet.

Too late. Someone was in the kitchen jostling around cups and stoking the fire. It must be the ever motherly May. Others started to move too, easing out of cramped positions on the floor.

What tack was Angelika to take? Henry was absent, he must be sleeping upstairs, so she didn't have him as a sounding board. It seemed the best way would be to ask innocently about the people up the road, which she did as soon as Roy stirred. He seemed to be leading everything that was going on.

When she did, he replied offhandedly. 'We banged on the door, but we got the usual yelling at to go away, they were fine. The water may not have got that far, the house is on the beginning of the rise in the land. One of us will pop up again later, but there's more important things to deal with.'

His boys joined him and nodded, what could she do? The children rushed downstairs, now excited by the night's event, and had to be discouraged from going out the front door. They were now rubbing the windows and squeaking in excitement. May came round with mugs of coffee and pieces of the ever present cake. Unorganised, everyone sat down at the table, as if in a sad reenactment of the previous night.

Roy stood up and, with authority, began issuing orders. 'We need to be organised now. Everyone needs to go home and check the houses. The water is receding slightly with the tide and we can get about with any of the four by fours and the tractors. I'm going to get the main digger. Ron and Pete, you'll need to sort out the milking. Honey and Poppy, you two need to check the chickens, hopefully they will still be roosting. They must be boxed up and put in the hayloft above the barn, it's well secured. The two pigs can come into the storeroom behind the dairy, which should be high enough to be out of the water.'

'Then we'll get all the heavy machinery and build the bank up again. There's a pile of hardcore behind the dairy, but if it's underwater, it'll be heavy. I'll see if I can get that machine working that's been here for years and I've never realised what it's use is. You know Ron and Pete, that thing with the hose on in the oldest shed. It's a water pump.'

'You'll never get all the water out with that, there's acres of land under water. Surely we just let it recede with the tide,' argued Pete.

'It's salt water, I want to get it off the fields as soon as possible. We'll take the bulldozer and clear the gap right open, so the water will drain away until low tide this afternoon. When as much as possible leaks away, we'll seal the bank and pump.' They nodded to that, yet Pete still muttered something about a fool's errand.

'We'll need some help with the little ones, we can't have them with us while we sort the chickens, Angelika, could you come up later and help? Angelika?'

Everyone was so engrossed in the conversation they hadn't seen Angelika put her fingers to her lips to keep the children quiet as she and Stew sneaked out of the door.

AFTERMATH

The coldness of the air struck her first, then the iciness of the water as she sank in it up to the tops of her legs. Stew swam with a bewildered expression on her face that made Angelika want to laugh, but they must get away from the café and find Dulcie and her mother. She turned to look back at the café as something was niggling at the back of her mind.

They had all woken up in the dry, no water inside, how on earth was that? Then it all made sense. Every house in Hamlet had a flight of steps leading up to them, they were built higher than the land level. How clever. The builders had known about the flooding, as each house now floated above the lapping sea water. Built to within inches of the highest tide, everyone's houses were safe and dry. Good, now all she needed to do was get up the lane, her house would be was fine, too.

Dragging Stew with her, she made it to her house, swung into the kitchen, and picked up her bag and keys. Hopefully, the Land Rover exhaust was out of the water and would start without any sucking any into the engine. Thank heavens for a short relationship with an off roader.

A bewildered Stew had to be heaved inside as the water was just on the edge of the cab, making it difficult to open the doors. Now to get up the lane and find out how Dulcie and Heather were doing. She wasn't going to be put off by being shouted at. Angelika carefully chugged up what she hoped was the lane, keeping to the side where there were the least potholes.

It was touch and go as sometimes she lurched and water poured into the cab. She could see the side of the lane because of the hedge, and that helped her keep on a good track.

The second crash had been Mark and Fiona's chimney. As she pased them, Henry's and the boys' housesseemed intact, although she saw missing tiles, and that was the same for the farmhouse, except bales and debris floated all around it.

It was uncanny with the floating houses and, as she passed the farm, her heart went out to Teresa and her drowned garden. At last, the old house came into sight and Angelika nearly jammed the brakes on in horror. The roof was completely gone, there weren't even any roof trusses left. She pushed her foot down and surged to what she guessed at the entrance, keeping to one side to avoid the pond. She stopped the engine and hoped it wouldn't flood. A wave of water in her wake surged past her.

'Dulcie, Heather, where are you?' she called from the cab.

There was no answer. She called and called, making her way to the house. Like the others, it was above the flood water, so she climbed up the steps to the front door and hammered. No answer, but she pushed, and the door opened.

It was dark and damp inside, where the rain must have poured in all night. Wallpaper hung off the walls, and the carpets were under an inch of water. She followed the dark corridor, pushing doors open to similar scenes of devastation, but part of her mind wondered if the house hadn't been in a bad state before.

As she stood in what must be the sitting

room, as there was a huge modern TV inside, she thought she heard a voice, so she froze. It came from the end of the corridor, so she squelched down. The door opened into the kitchen and there the two women huddled together. Both were bloodied, one looked up, it was Dulcie. All Angelika's first aid training flashed through her mind, she'd never had to use it before.

'Mother is hurt. She won't talk to me,' Dulcie said matter of factly, but with tears streaming down her face.

'What happened?'

Angelika got closer slowly, as she still wasn't sure what reception she would get from Heather.

'The roof blew away, and we were scared,' Dulcie continued, and moved over to show Angelika her mother.

'Hello Heather, can I see what's wrong?' There was no response.

Heather was grey haired, ashen, and unconscious. When Angelika gave her a pinch, she made no response. What now? Airway? She was clearly breathing, and her breath was warm on the back of Angelika's hand. Her circulation was ok too, as when she squeezed a finger, the colour soon returned. It must be just the head injury, which had clotted and was only bleeding a little.

'She's got a big cut, we will need to take her to hospital. How are you?' Angelika asked Dulcie in what she hoped was a kind voice.

'My arm won't work.'

Angelika saw it had bled and hung at a funny angle. 'We can get you and your mother sorted, Dulcie, but I need to get some help organised. Might there be some warm blankets somewhere?'

'In the airing cupboard on the stairs,' Dulcie

murmured.

Dulcie sank onto a chair and Heather lay still on the floor. The blankets were easy to find and Angelika wrapped the two up, she didn't know whether to give Dulcie something to drink as she may be dehydrated, but she might need an operation, so she didn't.

Would there be any signal yet? She rushed to the front door as there might be better reception there, and at last there was a bar on the screen of her phone. Dialling 999, she heard a vehicle in the distance, so she paused it. One of the farm's old trucks was swimming its way up the lane. Her heart ran cold in case it might be Roy or the boys and they might be obstructive in letting the women go to the hospital. To her relief, Glen was at the wheel.

'Good grief' were his first words as he saw the lack of roof. 'Are they alive?'

Angelika nodded.

'They sent me up here as there wasn't much I could do, it's total confusion with trying to sort livestock and tractors out. Roy sent an odd message, saying he will deal with the women and all you need to do is see they are ok. I don't know what problems Roy is so upset about, something is up with these two, but he sent these things to repair the house. I've got tarps, battens, and nails in the truck. Roy saw the damage from the farm. What is all the upset about?'

Angelika knew the message might also be a warning not to interfere, but she wasn't going to be threatened.

'I'm ringing 999, Heather has a bad head injury and Dulcie has a broken arm, they're both covered in blood.'

'Anything I can do?' Glen asked.

'Maybe see what needs doing on the roof? Don't go in as they don't know you.'

Glen smiled and strode off to the truck, at least he wore waders.

'Hello, ambulance please.'

The operator was kind and calm and talked Angelika through describing the injuries and what she needed to do.

'There's complete chaos here in the Bridmouth and coastal region. Trees down and flooding everywhere, electricity is off in many places too. We will need to take them to a hospital out of the area, so I'm passing you to the Search and Rescue helicopter, they're already airborne. I don't usually give all this information, but today isn't normal. The winchman, who is a paramedic, will come down, assess, and then use the stretcher to lift the patients. When you hear the helicopter, have someone ready to help with the cable, which will be dropped down first. They will take over and instruct you in what to do.'

Angelika went in and introduced Glen, who had unloaded the truck. She was now pale and drowsy, so didn't pay much attention. They had been told to find any ID for the women so they could be admitted. All they found was a large handbag, so they kept that ready.

RESCUE

The four of them sat and waited in an uneasy silence. Now she was warmed, Dulcie dozed off and the other two didn't want to talk and disturb her. After what seemed like hours, Glen looked up.

'Listen, I can hear something in the air.' He went out, ready to assist. The helicopter's engines became very loud as it hovered. Within minutes, a brightly dressed paramedic came in and began assessing. He was polite and professional and Angelika was relieved to have some of the weight lifted from her.

'We'll take the older lady first, do you have any information that might be useful for us?'

'I've not met her, but I've heard she's become aggressive and may have early symptoms of dementia. Dulcie here has Down's syndrome, but that's not a problem.' He understood, as he knew Dulcie was listening to every word they said and was watching what was going on.

Outside, the stretcher was lowered after much garbled communication. Angelika watched it through the kitchen window. Once inside, the unconscious Heather was strapped into it. Dulcie suddenly stood up, 'She always takes her handbag with her.' She thrust the old bag at them, and Glen put it inside the stretcher. Between them, they manhandled Heather out, and she swung into the air with the winchman.

When he returned, he bent down and talked in a calm voice. 'Now, Dulcie, we need to take you up to the helicopter, but first I must bandage your arm up a bit.'

'No. I want to stay here.'

At least she was more animated now, even if she was being mulish.

'Your mother is already on the helicopter and waiting for you,' he tried again.

'Don't want to go.'

At this point, Glen returned from the garden where he had gone to keep out of the way, accompanied by Roy. Angelika saw he was ashen with tiredness, he had aged in a day.

'What's going on here?' Roy sounded aggressive, and the paramedic looked up.

'These two ladies need to be in hospital, Dulcie here has a broken arm,' he replied in that calm voice.

'We look after our own here, they don't need to go.' Roy's voice was rising, clearly he was exhausted and getting irrational.

'Don't be ridiculous, they need medical help,' Angelika butted in.

'Don't be angry!' Dulcie suddenly shouted. 'I don't like you and I want to be with Mother.' She glared at Roy.

'Roy, you can't stop them,' interceded Glen, squaring up to him a bit. Angelika saw a glimpse of something in Roy's face, more than weariness on was it fear?

'Look Roy, Henry and I talked last night, it's all ok.' Sorry Henry, she said in her head. It was Roy's turn to go ashen, he turned and stalked out.

'Now young lady, will you come in my chariot?' asked the paramedic with a sudden grin and Dulcie finally let herself be prepared.

'Which hospital are you going to, we'll have to get out of here and follow you?' asked Glen.

'St Peter's, northwest London, it's the nearest to here that missed the storm. I can't see you getting out of here for a while, the road's blocked, we saw it from the air. We can't take any more on board. Sorry. Give me your contact details and I'll pass them on.' The other paramedic returned and Dulcie now lay quietly on the stretcher, tucked in and secured.

Glen and Angelika watched as it swung into the air. The paramedic waved a farewell, the helicopter turned and was gone with a roar.

CLEARING UP

'What now, Glen?' Angelika asked, wanting to throw herself into his arms.

He sank down against the side of his truck. 'I don't know, I'm exhausted and can't think straight. It was a flaming nightmare trying to get those animals moved, the storm had whipped them up into total stupidity. The horses nearly bolted down to the sea, we chased them in the vehicles. Once we got them through the fence and shut it, we heard the bank break through and the water came rushing in. I've never seen anything like it, and it was pitch dark, so it was all like a really bad black and white movie. We came back to the café on the tractor, which was just as well as all of May's picnic benches were washed inland and blocked the way. We bulldozed through the lot, they must all be ruined.'

'Then in daylight, after hardly any sleep, I waded down to the cottage although they were all shouting it was too dangerous. It's gone, Angelika, collapsed in a heap. It was a later build with no protection from anything, like the rest of the houses. Everything is either smashed or washed away.'

He rubbed his hands over a weary face.

'What about all your work stuff, the computers?'

'Oh, washed away too, no one will be able to use them. I've everything backed up on a server, there's no problem there, and they're insured. I'm simply sad as the house held so many memories.'

Angelika wanted to hug him, but didn't have the courage. Her feelings for him were really getting out of hand, but was it the emotion of the past day?

'What is Roy's problem? I've never seen him like that before,' he continued.

'Don't you know? Your family has had that house for years. I thought you were one of the extended family here.' Angelika was puzzled.

'Not been here long enough and I've been flitting backwards and forwards all the time.'

She told him a short version of the story.

When she had finished, he grinned, 'I always thought Henry had a misspent youth and there was some dark secret about these two. Well, it's all out in the open. Shall we do this roof and escape all the repercussions and stuff that will be going on?'

Lugging all the repair materials onto the roof was no easy matter. They found a way up through what had been the attic door. Trunks and suitcases lay on what had been the floor, so they dropped them down to the floor below. It was difficult, too, keeping to the rafters so that they didn't fall through the ceiling. Eventually the best job possible was done, with tarpaulin and wood keeping the wet away.

For a moment, they stood by the attic hatch and looked at the surrounding scenery. In the distance was the coastline, the calming sea, and along that on each side, the two seaside towns. Here in the middle stood Hamlet, the floating houses and the chapel which looked as though tiles had gone on the roof, but that would have to wait. By the beach, a busily working digger chugged away. It was the loudest thing they could hear; the seagulls hadn't returned yet.

There was something beautiful about the scene, but she couldn't describe it. Angelika prayed for God's help for everyone in this situation and felt guilty that she'd not even thought to pray before.

When they looked behind them, they saw fallen trees in the woods, blocking the track to the main road. It seemed that only the area around Hamlet was flooded.

'With this lie of the land, you would think that Hamlet was once an area used as saltings for literally making salt. It would explain why the houses are so high,' Glen remarked. 'Maybe the family made their fortune from it.'

'I wish I had enough battery to take a picture,' sighed Angelika, 'But there is a signal now, heaven's knows where from!'

'My phone's totally dead, so we're lucky yours had enough,' Glen grinned. 'Perhaps when they mend the roof, we can get a shot up here then,'

Inside, they shut the attic door, Glen securing it with wood and nails from being blown open.

'I can't resist a little look around, it's such a lovely old house,' he grinned mischievously.

'Go on then!'

There were three bedrooms, one clearly Dulcie's as it was decorated in pink, and cuddly toys lay everywhere. Heather's had a simple bed and wardrobe, very austere. The third was a playroom, and they were astonished at just how many toys Dulcie had, even if they were all neat and well used. The bathroom had a walk-in shower in a wet room, clearly new.

'They were being looked after,' remarked Angelika. 'Or were they being paid off?'

'Or holding Hamlet to ransom?'

'I hadn't thought of it like that, it would be a new slant. It would be from Heather though, Dulcie is a sweetie, no side to her at all,' Angelika smiled.

'So it's the evil stepmother, then?' Glen laughed.

'Could be, from what Dulcie has told me, Heather has always been a firm mother, but has been getting more and more angry. You've no doubt heard or seen how she reacts to anyone getting too close?'

'Indeed, she chucked a flowerpot at me once when I took their post in!'

Downstairs, the sitting room was filled with lovely but dilapidated, dirty furniture, rubbish was everywhere. The huge TV hung on the wall above the fireplace. A total contrast to the tidy bedrooms. The kitchen, filled with bits and pieces the paramedic had left behind, wasn't much better, and the blood everywhere didn't help.

'Should we clean it?' asked Glen.

'No!' Angelika was surprised by her vehemence. 'If things need to be changed in their lives, things must be left as they are for evidence.'

'I get you. Have you eaten today? It's nearly two and it will be high tide again, lets go and see how things are going with the pumping.' Glen made his way towards the door.

'Where will you stay tonight? I've a spare room if you don't fancy the café,' Angelika offered in desperation that he would leave her alone. She'd never felt like this before about anyone, she needed help, but God seemed to be letting her fathom this out on her own.

'I might well take you up on that. How do you think they milked all those cows with no electricity?' puzzled Glen.

'I should think they have a generator. I hope my exhaust isn't in the water, it might mean the Land Rover won't start.'

When they came out of the house, it was obvious the water had dropped. The track, although underwater, was visible. Both vehicles were well clear of it, started straight away. Stew, now dry, was ecstatic. Angelika realised the poor dog hadn't been fed all day.

Everyone was down at the beach, standing on the bank, watching the water drain away almost as fast as it had come in. Even the usually immaculate Teresa had donned a boiler suit and looked mucky.

'See, I knew it would work,' were Roy's triumphant words to the pair. 'We'll shore it up as soon as the tide gets too high, pump and then when it goes out again, open up again and let it drain.' He looked almost manic but made no references to Dulcie and Heather.

'How are Dulcie and Heather?' asked May, so Angelika told them all. It was clear that now they all knew that she knew, Angelika had the sense that they were just expecting her to go along with things. Perhaps that would be best for the moment.

'Are all the animals safe?' She changed the subject.

'Yes, most of the chickens are in the barn attic. Cattle and ponies are fine,' answered Pete. 'How much salt has got into the ground is another matter. We might get away with it as this all used to be marshland, but we might have no good grazing for a couple of years. Time will tell.'

'We've lost all of our crops, even the roots

have come out of the ground. They must be spread over the whole estate.' Angelika was sure no one missed the desperation in Fiona's voice.

'Nothing salvageable?' she asked.

'No, but we were at the end of the season, we should get by until spring,' Mark was more upbeat.

'Now, let's not be gloomy!' May butted in with her usual bossiness and love. 'We've cooked a huge stew on the aga and we all need to eat. There's a couple of hours before high tide and you start playing with the toys again, so come and eat.'

There was still no electricity, but they had water to wash, and soon they all sat down to eat. Stew and the dogs were fed together, so Angelika didn't have to deal with her for a while. It was a different sort of meal compared to the previous night; the fun had gone, even though pudding was more of the enormous cake.

Henry had insisted on going home and was doing what he could to rescue the bees, who also fortunately had been high enough on their stands to stay dry, but they weren't happy. The girls had occupied the children who had insisted on seeing that their ponies were ok and likewise were now being fed.

There was a weariness and tiredness in the group, and there was bickering about why no one had checked the forecast the day before. Apparently, there had been plenty of storm warnings in the media. Glen and Angelika shared glances and, at the earliest opportunity, left. They had offered help earlier on, but it wasn't wanted, things were under control. It just needed the electricity to come back on.

The water was under welly height now, even if it still covered everywhere. Stew splashed about with joy at going home, and once in the garden, began to bark. There, looking disgusted at the salty water, were the ducks, who quacked a begrudging welcome.

Angelika fetched them a large bucket of grain, which was stored in the old, waterproof freezer. The floor of the shed was now dry, so she left the feeder there with a bucket of fresh water from the water butt. She watched the ducks devouring their meal, and later, from the kitchen window, saw them fly away, certainly to somewhere less salty.

Inside, she gave Glen some bedding and left him to get the spare room sorted. There hadn't been much left in her fridge anyway, but they found some bread in the freezer and chose the tins from Mary and Phil's largesse. The house felt cold without heating; it had caught the damp of the flooding. They lit the fire in the sitting room and sat there watching the flames, not really knowing what to do or talk about except yawn. They had one lamp leant to them by May, but that would have to be used sparingly, as the supply of oil was limited. Tiredness was overwhelming, and Angelika was trying to think how to say she wanted to go to bed, when at the same time she wanted to stay with him. They both jumped out of their skins as Angelika's phone rang. She'd thought it was dead.

'This is St Peter's hospital. I understand you helped in the rescue of Mrs Smith and her daughter?' In her tiredness, Angelika nodded, and the voice continued, anyway.

'They are on the ward now, we needed to keep them together as Dulcie was getting distressed when we tried to separate them. I'm just doing the paperwork. For her mother, Heather Smith, there is no problem. But for Dulcie, we have no record under that surname, no NHS number, nothing, nor under the one she insists is hers, which is that she's Lady Hutton. She's getting very confused. Is Smith her mother's maiden name?'

Oh, the proverbial had hit the fan and why should she have to sort this out? Roy, May, or Henry should deal with this, but how could they?

'I'm sorry, I've only been here a short time and know nothing about this. Is it really going to be a problem for her treatment?'

'No, of course not. But if they have any further family, it would be helpful if we can contact them. It's as if Dulcie doesn't exist. Mrs Smith can't help, as she's unconscious. She may not come around for days.' Angelika now realised she had no idea how the injuries had occurred either, she'd never thought to ask.

'As far as I understand, Mrs Smith has looked after Dulcie since she was born, her mother died. They're not related. I understand there are no living relatives on either side.' Would that do?

'We'll just have to do our best then. Will you be visiting, maybe you could check their house for letters or things?'

'I'll see what I can do.'

The line went dead.

'Did you hear that, Glen?'

'Just hospital admission, they'll be fine,' he mumbled.

Then, as it was getting dark, they went to their bedrooms and slept like the dead until the next morning, when the electricity coming back on made many beeps as things rebooted and the freezer chugged back into life.

REPERCUSSIONS

Angelika peered blearily over her cup at Glen.

'What happens now do you think?'

'I guess they'll be opening the gap again to get the last of the water out, I heard that pump as I dozed off, and it was still humming this morning. They must all be exhausted,' he yawned in reply.

Their phones were charged again, so they both spent time fiddling about with them. Messages came, summoning them both to brunch at the café, and to bring any thawed out things to share. Stew bounced around, insisting that now she'd breakfasted, she needed her walk.

Outside, it was another beautiful day, as if in compensation for the storm. Stew splashed about happily but was clearly annoyed that she couldn't find anywhere dry to poop. Angelika wondered where she had done it for the past couple of days, it didn't bear thinking about. Eventually, she found a patch by the greenhouse and she rushed around again in relief. There was no sign of the ducks, but Angelika put fresh grain and water down. In the garden, she was just able to see the outline of the pond.

'I'm going down to see if anything can be salvaged from my cottage,' Glen stated.

'Do you need any help?' Angelika wondered what she would do with herself, and wanted to

137

go with him, rather than stay in the house on her own.

'No. It'll be heaving stuff about, I'll manage.' He grinned and his face changed. 'Thanks for letting me stay, can I book tonight?'

'Of course, and hot baths might be on the menu this evening, the tank takes ages to heat up.' Angelika really didn't like showers, and tried not to think a totally wrong thought about sharing a bath with him. She was both appalled and laughing at herself for feeling like the lovesick teenager she had once been.

'Consider me booked!' With a sudden dart, he kissed her on the cheek and was gone. Angelika wandered back indoors to check her fridge and freezer, touching her face, feeling blessed.

Loaded with bits and pieces of food that needed eating, Angelika was paddling her way through the rapidly receding water when she heard a strange rumbling in the distance. Looking up the lane, she saw the familiar sight of the milk lorry making its way to the farm. They had access to the world again. As she looked, behind it came an electricity board van and several other work vehicles. Freedom!

She took herself to the café with the good news. May, who stood at the door looking at the workers, seemed weary and took the offerings with thankfulness.

'Now, at least we'll all be able to get out and shop. The water is going down so fast. Once the internet is up, Roy and the boys can get on to the authorities to get that wall re built for once and for all, it's been a weak point for years. And we'll be living in mud till this dries out. I hope the forecast for dry weather is correct.'

At that point, more vehicles rumbled down, with trailers laden with hard core and steel girders.'

'I just hope there will be grants he can apply for, all that stuff isn't cheap.' May sounded worried.

'Surely the government or EU will supply grants, global warming and all that stuff?'

'Maybe, but in the meantime, Roy's paid for it all.'

An idea was forming in the back of Angelika's mind, then the gang of children arrived, sloshing happily through the increasingly muddy water, and May put her happy face on.

'Right you lot, what have you brought for the feast? Not more eggs, I hope.'

Before long, everyone was back again at the table in the café. The milk had been taken away, although some had been lost because the tanks had been full. The deliveries for repairing the wall had been stowed and one cheerful bloke had told them the net was back up again.

There was not only a sense of relief but also exhaustion from everyone, and Angelika knew it wasn't a good time to relay her news, but it had to be said. No one had mentioned Dulcie and Heather or asked about them.

'Umm, I need to ask you all something.' Boy, was she nervous.

'I had a phone call from the hospital, and they are having trouble with tracking Dulcie down. Was her birth never recorded? For Heather, who is unconscious, they have her NHS details and things, but nothing for Dulcie. She is insisting she is Lady Hutton, and they are confused with the different surnames, as she's also insisting that Heather is her mother. Why should she say that? What has Dulcie herself been told?'

The older ones shifted in their seats and looked uncomfortable.

'Also, none of you have even asked me how they are getting on or even asked what happened. Don't you care?' Angelika perceived her voice was rising, but she was still tired and it boiled over as anger. 'I know you've all been stressed, but even so...'

'We've cared for those two for so many years, you have no idea! Bustling in with your do-goodyness. Never seen you do any real churchy stuff. They have taken so much from us, those two, like we are serfs. Have you seen that wet room?' Teresa exploded. 'We all paid for that.'

'But you all want to keep your houses and land, or are you all too scared that if you make it official and put yourselves on the deeds from your bits of paper that someone will emerge and take them from you? Or are the pieces of paper not legal, or did you write them yourselves?' Angelika was warming up.

'How long ago was all this? Surely it was binding? Did none of you research things now we have the net? You all just wanted to live in your little ruts. You could have helped Dulcie to live a more normal life. Helped Heather with hers. Did any of you make friends with her? She must have been lonely. How on earth have you lived in this nightmare for so long?'

'Look, it wasn't us, it was that older lot that got the houses,' snapped Honey, much to Angelika's surprise. 'With the amount of money they've had, we would have had new cars and other things. Now you come in here and judge us, we don't even know if you really are a relative of Phil.'

'I had to give the solicitor all my ID documents.'

'A DNA test would sort this all out,' Poppy countered.

'But Phil is dead,' Angelika countered back.

'You could've found some hair or something in the house.'

The argument escalated, with everyone throwing it all at Angelika, until with a huge roar, Henry stopped them all.

'We don't know who you are Angelika but at the same time, my generation has been guilty of living a lie. It would be good to be free of this and live without guilt. Many times we have talked about going to a solicitor and we have talked ourselves out of it. We buried a woman all those years ago, and did nothing about it, acting like some sort of secret society. It is time to change things. Once all this mess from the storm is cleared up, we will, but give us some breathing space first.'

That caused more heated discussion and Angelika sensed it was time to leave in the face of all this hostility about her that was being bandied about.

Glen suddenly stepped in with a roar as well. 'Hey! I had no idea at all about this, my parents never said a word. So this is the community fund I've been asked to donate to so many times? I'm ashamed to own what's left of our place. I will sort this out. I'm off to London this afternoon.'

That shut them up.

'Now, I've got some more to say to you,' Angelika was still furious, but calmer. She had something else to throw at them. 'I never wanted Phil's estate, but I have found real peace and joy living here with you, and it hurts so much to think how you have been hiding your true feelings about me. Just to show you how I am genuine, I have something for you. I have a lot of money from Phil that I don't need and don't want. I can give this to charity, or I can give it to you. Fiona and Mark need to rebuild their business, Teresa, her garden, there are repairs to houses like the broken chimneys, hen houses need rebuilding, the sea wall needs money too. I bet none of you could get house insurance, I haven't. I will pay for these things, then I will leave and sell the house to someone who will love it. At least I have ownership, even if the roots are another piece of paper. I really thought I was welcome here, but I was wrong. And still, not a single one of you has asked how Dulcie and Heather are, shame on you.'

With that, she pushed her chair back and strode out, ignoring any remarks that were being thrown at her. Outside, she found Stew at her side, wagging her tail fiercely in consternation. The door banged and Glen stood beside her.

'Want a lift to London, I'm going anyway?'

LONDON

They drove part of the way deep in thought. Angelika had collected bags and thrown them into the back of Glen's car, which he had brought down to the seafront. It was filled with possessions, pictures, and pieces of computer, all of which he had rescued from the rubble of the cottage. Stew sat in the front, happy to be in the adventure, not knowing that Angelika hadn't had the courage to ask someone to look after her. The ducks had more food in the shed than even they had the stomachs for, it would do for a good few days. Angelika didn't even know if or when she would return.

As they crossed the cattle grid, they entered another country. So many felled trees, now sawn away to clear the road, made her feel like she had lost all sense of direction. The nearer they got to Bridmouth, the damage became more visible in tarpaulin'd and damaged houses, roots of trees and teams working to repair infrastructure. It was only as they left the coast and hit the motorway that things got back to normal.

It had been an odd sensation, leaving Hamlet after what seemed like forever. It was like something lifted with each mile, and it gave Angelika a new perspective on everything. What a mess everyone had been in with that hold over their lives.

There lay an evil shadow over everything, whether conscious or not. She had bought into it, with her unacknowledged need to be accepted into a community, a family. She had let them use her and made the excuse of showing her love rather than telling them about God's love and doing her job. Even if God didn't need her as a pastor, as a Christian, she had a duty to tell people about him. Angelika was deeply ashamed and sat in a well of self pity until Glen broke in.

'Penny for them?'

'I'm beating myself up for not doing more when I moved in.'

'How?' Glen was puzzled.

'Oh, just that I wasn't doing my job as a pastor should do, and I let myself get sucked in with all their cover-ups. Have you ever heard a more unlikely story?'

'I know, if I hadn't seen their house and heard all their explanations, I wouldn't have bought it either. My parents never told me a thing and left the cottage in their will as if all was in order. I don't even remember any paperwork about it. My grandparents were hippy types about Henry's age, but they've all gone now and there's no one to ask. It's a relief to leave it all. I've rescued most of the precious stuff from the cottage,' Glen sounded pleased.

'Does that mean you're not going back?' Angelika's flagging spirits drooped even lower.

'Well, maybe not until the spring. I have the boat and a hankering to do a long trip in her. Did I tell you I sold my business when I was in the US? I've enough money to keep me going for years and even longer if I'm careful. But I can't see myself not working, I'm too much of a workaholic. The storm has proved that I don't need bricks and mortar. I've a small flat in Leytonstone. You're welcome to stay, but it will be the sofa.'

'Thanks, but I have friends who I know will

put me up.' That was so tempting, but she ran away from it. 'If you will drop me there, that would be great. Then I will go to the hospital with some flowers and things, all from everyone at Hamlet. I can't help pondering about it all. Why does Dulcie call Heather Mother when she isn't?'

'It's all most odd. It crossed my mind too, that as there are no records of Dulcie's birth, and maybe where they didn't register Veronica's death either, that a long-lost relative might turn up at any time and claim that place.'

'Did you know Veronica is buried in the chapel graveyard?'

'Good grief, no, of course not, it gets worse and worse. How could they let this dark secret go on? It's becoming like one of those murder mysteries on TV, when we get back, you might be next on the list!' Glen spluttered with laughter. 'Now, seriously, would you really give them all that money after what you know?'

'I expect I will, the idea was at the back of my mind after something May said. They don't deserve it, but that's the message of the Gospel,' Angelika said carefully.

Glen snorted, and they changed the subject to talk about what they were looking forward to the most now they were in civilisation. To their mutual surprise, they both wanted a greasy, hot burger and chips, so once in the suburbs of London, they drove to the first drive in place they found. Stew was delighted.

Glen cheered Angelika up as they chatted about so many random subjects as they battled through the London streets, finding they had very similar senses of humour. They agreed to meet in a couple of days so Glen could find out about the situation with Dulcie and Heather.

The smell and sound of London was a shock after the quietness of the countryside. She took it all in as she waited for her friends to answer the door. Brian and Sue were old buddies in the Salvation Army, who ran an open door house for friends, and so they greeted her with much love and hugs when they saw her. Over a cup of tea, she explained the situation to them fully. Stew loved the house as she got treats aplenty, so Angelika had no qualms when she left her with them to visit the hospital.

IN THE HOSPITAL

Angelika had always thought that large hospitals were like worlds of their own, and when inside for a long time, it would be possible to feel like the world outside didn't exist any longer. St Peter's was no different. She tried to follow a confusion of ward signs, lines on the floors, endless lifts, stressed visitors and over busy nurses. The antiseptic air also reminded her of times when she'd had to do official visits, whether for new life or old going heavenwards.

Finally, she found the ward she wanted and the nurses' station. She was giving all her information when there came a shriek and she was engulfed in a Dulcie hug, albeit one handed, as her arm was heavily plastered.

'I knew you would come. I've been praying for it to be soon.' She stood back and grinned. Angelika now saw a large, fading bruise on her face. She didn't know how to ask about this, so let it be.

'You must be Miss Jones, we spoke on the phone. Did you manage to find that information?' A tall nurse with a gentle grin stood there with a clipboard, Angelika sensed she wouldn't go into details in front of Dulcie and was touched by that.

'Mrs Smith has regained consciousness, but we haven't been able to glean much more.' She turned to her side. 'It's about where you live,

Dulcie.'

'Oh, Mother knows all that, come and meet her Angelika and have a talk.' Dulcie was pulling Angelika away from the nurse, who simply grinned and nodded.

In a side ward, an older lady, who could only be Heather, with lanky hair sticking out of a huge head bandage, was sitting up in bed, furiously pushing at a remote control for the overhead TV.

'I can't believe it's run out so soon, Dulcie, I'll have to send that nice porter to the cash machine again. Oh, who are you?' She glared at her visitor.

'Hi, I'm Angelika, Dulcie's friend from Hamlet.'

'Oh, the one in the church?'

'Yes, indeed, Dulcie has a wonderful voice.'

With that, the woman's face changed. 'Call me Heather. Yes, she does. If she had mastered reading music, she could have been in the Bridmouth choir. Come and tell me what has happened. Dulcie has told me her version, but that was limited by our accident.'

That was interesting, maybe now she would get to hear exactly what had happened. Dulcie plopped down on the bed and her mother winced as the bed shook.

Angelika sat on the hard hospital chair and cleared her throat.

'The storm took everyone in Hamlet by surprise, and the strength of it was incredible.'

'Not us, Dulcie and I watched the news at

lunchtime and saw all sorts of warnings, but no one came here to see how we were prepared,' Heather sniffed.

'We were having a birthday party in the café,' Angelika continued.

'Didn't ask us.'

She ignored that.

'The sea wall broke and flooded everywhere, the electricity went off. The wind knocked off most of the chimneys and your roof. Roy said they banged on the door, but you told them you were fine. Then the roof must have gone during the night. I found you in the morning and we called 999. They took you away in a helicopter.'

'I can remember that, I flew. I wasn't scared,' Dulcie announced with a grin. 'And the nice man inside tied my arm up and gave me medicine.'

'I don't remember a thing except being the kitchen and the storm,' said Heather.

'Yes, you do. You got cross when they banged on the door, and when I went to open it, you grabbed my arm and twisted it so it wouldn't work anymore,' said Dulcie in an annoyed, loud voice.

'Dulcie, that's not the sort of thing you tell strangers.'

She burst into tears. 'Then I hit you with the saucepan because it hurt and you were cross with me again.'

'Do you often do things like this?' Angelika burst out.

'No,' they both shouted at once.

'It was the strain and fear of the storm and I have been under the weather lately,' Heather explained.

'Is that why you are always cross with everyone?'

'Dulcie, please, that's enough.' Heather certainly sounded cross now.

'Sorry.' Dulcie folded her arms and frowned.

'Why don't you finish that lovely picture you were doing of the storm and sea that's on the cupboard over there and Angelika and I can have a chat.'

With a grumpy face, Dulcie obeyed and yet soon became totally engrossed with her pens.

'I'm sorry you had to hear that. We did have a fight, but it's the only time that's ever happened, I was so scared we would be washed away.'

'So why didn't you accept their offer of help?'

'It sounds silly, but I was scared to go out. I've found it a problem lately,' Heather looked down, avoiding eye contact.

'So she did you a favour whacking you over the head, then?'

Heather had the grace to smile. To Angelika, it didn't seem that she was that demented, daft and bossy, yes, but she was no expert.

'How's your head now?'

'Dulcie didn't crack it, but it's really sore. The pain killers are good though. Look, she hasn't been scribbling for five minutes and she's asleep already. She feels safe with us both here and has relaxed. I wish I could have some of what they give her. It's as if I've run out of sleep.'

Angelika grinned in agreement, looking at Dulcie sprawled over the table.

'Now she's out for the count, I want to have a chat. You see, she talks about you all the time. I haven't been down to the church as I said, sometimes I find it difficult to go outside these days. She says you're a real church pastor?'

Angelika nodded.

'I must tell you some things which Dulcie partially knows about, and others that are best she doesn't. Would this be like a confessional, and remain private? I don't want all the praying stuff.'

'If you so wish.'

'I do, but maybe they will need to be told in the future and if Dulcie and I are gone, it won't matter anyway. Can you pass me that cup, my mouth's dry?' She took a large gulp as if buying time.

SECRETS

'Right, that lot down the lane may have told you their side to the story, so it's about time my side is told. Back in the 1960s – yes, I am that old, don't look it, do I?'

Angelika had to nod and grin once more.

'Those were great days for the young who didn't carry wounds of the war. I was fifteen when I got my job in London and walked out of school into the biggest party ever. It was all centred around the Dustbin Club. You've heard this bit?'

Again, she nodded.

'I had such fun, but was blissfully ignorant of the facts of life, and I learnt quickly the hard way. One summer weekend, it got about that there was to be a big party in the country and a lot of the members of the club were going. I hitched a lift down in the back of someone's mini. We had a ball. Wine and drugs, interesting things to smoke and fantastic music. It was great, no neighbours or anyone to interfere.'

'The party carried on into the week and no one went home. I hadn't been paid and so had no means of getting back to London unless I hitched or someone else was driving. So I stayed, it was no hardship and my job was as good as gone, but there would be others.'

'Later in the week, things calmed down, we swam, took walks in the country, talking about life and God and all sorts of daft things.' Her eyes were far away, reminding Angelika of Henry.

'The parties began again, and one weekend the woman who seemed to be running it began to behave oddly. She was handing out gifts and letters to people, as if trying to give everything she had away. I noticed that she had a large tummy and having been around in my huge family when another sibling arrived, guessed what was happening. With a couple of others who weren't quite so stoned, we got her upstairs and into one of the bedrooms. This all took part in the house I live in now, did I say?'

'Before long, without much screaming, she had a little girl, and it was all love and peace and partying for the newborn. I stayed with her and kept an eye on the baby. Then Veronica began to bleed. Not like a period bleed, but lots. I screamed for help, but the music was too loud and everyone was out of it. In the end, I dragged a few of them upstairs, but none of them would phone for a doctor; the line had been cut off in the house, anyway. No one would help, let alone listen to me. I got towels and tried to stop the flow. She got weaker and weaker and then passed away. I was only fifteen, what was I supposed to do?'

'In the morning, when they all sobered up, I got through to them. That made them open their eyes. They still wouldn't get a doctor or the police, but called a meeting of about ten of them who were there all the time. Do you know what they did? The next night, they crept down to the church, dug a hole and buried her, no service, nothing. The church wasn't used, so there wouldn't be a problem with a vicar discovering what they had done.'

'Then it dawned on them that they had to sort things out and what about the baby? I insisted that one of them with a car went and got all the things that a baby needs, bottles, the lot. They had to have a whip round, but at last the baby, who was a little poppet and so quiet, had a feed. I sort of slipped into looking after her.'

'This ended all the partying, and most of them skulked shamefacedly back to town. The ones left remaining talking about forming a commune, as it seemed she had left them some houses in the little village. Without asking me, they presumed I would stay and look after the baby. Over the next couple of weeks, they took themselves off to these houses, leaving us alone.'

'They came later with money and food and kept me going, but then left me in this house, all alone with a baby that wasn't mine. I expect you've been told their version of all this?' she asked again.'

Angelika was getting well versed at nodding, it seemed that was all she needed to do.

'A year slipped by, then another, and I kept on saying I would go back and leave them, but I couldn't. I've never left. The baby grew, and it was clear she wasn't right. We didn't have all these social services then as we have now, and with the mother not there, what should I do? I couldn't face the thought of putting the baby into an institution.'

'It wasn't so bad, as she grew, we had tutors for her to give her skills and she played with children in the commune. Mary was one of her friends, but they grew apart as Mary grew up and Dulcie didn't. Roy was her special pal, but he wouldn't admit it now. I did get a car and had a bit of a life, but a single mother with a bastard, disabled baby isn't at the top of any social ladder.'

'A few years later, I did a degree with the OU, but never found a way to leave her and go to work. Their guilt kept us well supplied, but as the years have passed and those children had children, the memories faded and with that, the wanting to support us. To many, we were just a dead weight they resented paying for.'

'We get on well together, but my days are numbered and I'm not leaving it to them to sort out Dulcie's fate. I'm not asking you to have her, but maybe be a supporter of her. It's worrying me that we had that fight, it has never happened before, but what if it does? She's so innocent and vulnerable, even if she does get stubborn and bad tempered. Have I been such a bad mother over the years?'

'There have been a lot of comments to me that you are nasty, turn on people and can't be trusted.' It had to be said, and Angelika felt there was more to come.

'I know, I know.' Heather sighed and looked at the gently snoring Dulcie.

'About five years ago, there was a visitor to Hamlet. Oh no, it won't sound right without you knowing the whole truth. I can't go on living this lie. I'm hoping you will understand and that you won't run away from me.' There was both hysteria and panic in her voice. She now wept as she spoke. 'I've never told anyone this, you are the first, so I'm having to put my trust in you, the repercussions are huge.'

'The little baby, despite all I did, and the books I read, didn't thrive. They wouldn't let me go to a doctor, but came up with all sorts of quack remedies.'

'I had a problem, too. I hadn't been exactly pure, and before I left London, I'd had a short but very sweet affair with a sailor, who said he loved me and then sailed away down the Thames. It became clear that there was a consequence of it and I was pregnant. I gave up all the pills, booze and pot, but even so, I think they are to blame for how she is, that's made another load of guilt upon me. Not that anyone there noticed anything. Like Veronica, I gave birth on my own, but this time, all went well. Do you understand what I'm telling you? My daughter arrived just after Veronica's died and I'm guilty of burying that little one next to her mother in the little graveyard. Please don't judge me, it's all done.'

Angelika's mind was working overtime, so she let Heather go on.

'No one noticed the swap, far less cared. I lived a lie and took from them, when really I should have admitted it, left and gone home. Many times over the years, especially as things have deteriorated, I've wanted to leave. I made plans, yet never had the courage to carry them out. But no one in Hamlet ever befriended me, I was a nuisance and I think they deserved it. I've saved a little, and now I could claim various benefits. Maybe I am just a lazy parasite.'

'Five years ago, Mary came back from a holiday with a new husband. I didn't see him at first, just heard about it and was pleased for her. Until I saw him. He was Phil, my lover, Dulcie's father.'

There she stopped and the two women sat in silence for a while to the gentle snoring. Angelika's thoughts were on a crazy merry go round.

'What would you have done if she had been a boy? So that's why she calls you mother and yet herself Lady Hutton. Did she never ask you why you had different names?'

Heather ignored the first question and shook her head. 'Things were different then, and details were simply not spoken about. The children never used her surname. When she was older and we tried to teach her to write, it never crossed her mind, and she never read anyway. Dulcie didn't realise we had different names. I don't think she would have understood if I had told her. So I am simply Mother in her eyes as she never saw anything else in me.'

'That's why she has no record, you never registered the birth like the two deaths. Good grief, what a mess,' Angelika snapped, but Heather continued oblivious.

'Phil didn't recognise me. I rushed out onto the track to talk to him, but he blanked me beyond a good afternoon and was gone. I rushed after him, but he just got angry and said he'd never met me before. I don't know if that was a lie or truth. After that I began a sad time, wrote letters to him I never posted.'

'I got angry with the people of Hamlet, got more and more demanding, and couldn't get out of that front door. That's the situation you walked into. I can't see how to resolve it, I guess I'll be sent to prison. But Dulcie must be looked after. I'll understand if you hate me now, but please don't tell anyone unless they are the law.

'This is a total catastrophe, and I'll have to ask you not to hate me, too,' Angelika said with a sob in her voice.

Heather peered at her with a puzzled face.

'It looks like I might be Dulcie's half sister.'

MORE AFTERMATH

Heather looked at her in complete astonishment. 'How on earth did you get to that?'

'I was left the house as Mary has no children, several people have told me so. Why would they have left it to me if there was no family connection? It's been puzzling me the whole time I've been here, and this makes sense. There's no way we'll ever find out with them both dead. I've had it thrown at me that I should do a DNA test with some of Phil's things from the house, but there hasn't exactly been time. Do you have any pictures of him? There are none in my house.'

Heather peered closely at her. 'No. But as I look at you, I can see a likeness between you, same eyes and build.'

Angelika saw tears welling up again in Heather's eyes when she talked about Phil being dead. Poor woman. The two sat in silence for a while and the full implications of all Heather had said began to rumble through Angelika's head. It meant that Heather, for most of her life, had sponged off what she now called the commune. That her whole life had been a lie. She could have packed her bags and gone home at any time.

But would you fight for your disabled child to get the best in a world that hadn't yet taken on illegitimate babies and the disabled? Was it easy to get in such a rut? It seemed Dulcie didn't know, especially as she insisted on calling herself Lady Hutton, so how would that work out if she was told the truth?

'I've done a terrible thing, haven't I?' Heather said, echoing Angelika's very thoughts.

'I'm not here to condemn you. We all make mistakes. But I can't see how the people of Hamlet can find this out without there being the most almighty uproar, maybe court cases and worse.'

'But they hid Veronica's death in the first place. If I hadn't carried on with the deception all those years, where would they be?' Heather almost snapped.

Better off and possibly have real ownership of the place, but Angelika didn't speak the thought aloud. 'Did you never think of going home?'

'Often. And several times I packed up to go. But when I wrote home once, the letter came back, unknown at this address, and that was only a couple of years later. I lost all my courage and couldn't face their anger.'

A new idea formed in Angelika's mind, it wasn't going to show God's grace as she had originally thought, but it might work in the same way. She put that aside for later.

Dulcie stirred and smiled at them.

'You've had the best sleep since it all happened,' Heather smiled.

'My arm still hurts.'

'Let's talk to the doctor when he comes around.'

The subject was firmly closed, so as it was nearly their supper time, Angelika left, promising to return in the morning. As she walked down the quiet corridor, she heard pounding footsteps behind her, and stood to one side to let the emergency pass. It didn't. Behind her was an elderly, bespectacled doctor, his coat and tie all askew.

'I'm sorry, were you visiting Mrs Smith and her adopted daughter?'

'Yes, I'm not a relative, but what do you want?' Adopted?

'I'm Dr Evans, the bone doctor,' he sniggered, as he was obviously used to the joke. 'Come and sit with me in the café for a minute.'

Mystified, she followed him down the corridor and waited while he bought them coffees.

He plonked down two cups that spilt and cut straight to the chase. 'I'm not only a doctor but also I'm a historian, and when I saw Dulcie's name on the sheet, I was astonished. The last of the Hutton family disappeared in the 1960s. They were a family that played a much unheard of part in our country's history. It was James Hutton in the times of Charles the second that began the family's involvement with the royal family… Oh, I've done it again, haven't I?' He had seen Angelika begin to switch off, as clearly many people did.

'I've been researching the family history as a lifelong project since I was at university. When I saw Dulcie's name, I thought someone was making a joke, but she insisted it was true and to ask her mother, who agreed, but with the point that she is actually Dulcie's lifelong carer. In one sense I was overjoyed, but on examining the x-rays and looking closely at Dulcie's hands, I knew immediately something wasn't right.'

'There is a longstanding family genetic trait that runs only through the women. It means that the third finger and toe turn inwards. It's so marked that it shows up on x-rays, even if the digit outwardly is only mildly twisted. Dulcie carries no such trait.'

'But she has Down's, won't that affect it?' This was a nightmare.

'No, there have been a few, um, slightly disabled members of the family, and they all carry it. I have read the diaries of Lady Jane Hutton who lived in the 1870s, and she talks about it at length.'

'Are there truly none of the family left, even the wrong side of the blanket?' Angelika was clutching at straws.

'None that I've found, and I've done the family tree for years, even before the jolly old net made things much easier.'

'So what are you going to do?'

'What? Nothing. It's been a lifelong search and to have one's hopes dashed, that one relative is left is a total blow. I just wanted to see if you could shed some light on this.'

'Is there money in the estate?' Angelika realised she was deflecting, but she had to know, and she tried to think of how she was going to go on with this conversation.

'No, it was all blown by the last daughter, Veronica, who disappeared shortly after her mother died. The estate itself had long been sold, and the house demolished after the war. There was nothing left.'

He doesn't know about Hamlet? Angelika hoped her body language or eyes weren't giving anything away.

'Have you ever been down to see what remains of the house?' she asked.

'Once years ago, but all I found was some bricks in a cattle field and got chased away by some hippie yelling it was a private commune and to get lost.'

Relief flooded over Angelika. It was only

Dulcie's immediate identity that needed to be sorted. But how? She slurped her coffee to gain thinking time.

'I don't know how I can help you. I only helped with getting them rescued after the storm,' was the best she could do.

'There is the coincidence of the name and that they lived near where the estate lay. I thought that by some freak chance, I had found a relative. Mrs Smith isn't very forthcoming about things.' He was like a dog with a tasty bone.

'Dulcie wouldn't be able to help you, even if she could. Maybe she saw the name in the church. Down's people can have vivid imaginations and she was on her own a lot,' Angelika offered.

'There's a church?' He nearly jumped off his seat. 'That was always a puzzle to me, why they didn't have a chapel in the house, or a church nearby. The estate didn't run too close to the sea as the old saltings often flooded, so I never searched in them. I must go down there soon and have a look. I expect you are right about her imagining things, Mrs Smith said the same thing.'

He changed the subject.'It will be a bit of a fiddle, but in the meantime I can update the NHS system, even though we can't find any records of Dulcie's birth. I expect there was some sort of cock up. I'll ask Mrs Smith for her date of birth.'

Angelika, for once in her life was unable to say anything. Help! The most effective prayer ever.

'I wouldn't go down there too soon, as there is a lot of damage from the storm. I have a house down there, you'd be welcome to stay while you investigate,' she blurted out.

Where had that come from? Then she knew. There was a purpose and plan in all this. This was a

God incidence, her name for coincidences that ran all through her life.

Dr Evans beamed. She couldn't help but think he was in the wrong profession, he should have been a university historian.

'Let's exchange phone numbers and emails, and we'll keep in touch,' she continued.

'Marvellous. In the meantime, I can examine my maps and find out more about that area. I'll look at it all from a different angle.' His eyes were far away, then they snapped back to the present. 'Dulcie's arm is a straightforward break, fortunately in the lower arm where it's less difficult to heal than the upper arm. It won't need pinning. She could go home now if she had somewhere to go to.' He was all the professional doctor again as they finished their coffees and rose to leave.

Angelika realised that Heather and Dulcie might have to stop living the lie, as their house may be no longer habitable. But that was for another day. Tomorrow she was going to get to know her sister properly.

Brian, Sue and Stew eagerly awaited her return, and it was a relief to plop on their comfy sofa and then tell them the entire story, with its twists and turns and revelations over a supper of spaghetti Bolognese and wine.

'That is the most incredible story. Are you going to tell Dulcie you are her sister, or will you wait for some confirmation? Why don't you contact that solicitor?' Brian asked.'

'I might well do that, but for the moment, I'm going to err on the side of caution and wait for things to unfold. I can get to know her better, and that is enough. She's never been to London or even a big city. Her clothes are awful, and she's not even that plump. We'll shop for a whole new look.'

They then spent some time praying into the situation, thanking God for bringing the blessing of sisterhood, but also asking for guidance on how this situation could be resolved. What would he have them do? They took their authority, and commanded love and forgiveness into everyone's hearts, to change things in God's way, not that of the world.

SHOPPING WITH DULCIE

The hospital didn't seem so grim the next morning, and it was with glee that Angelika asked Dulcie if she would like to go shopping. Her face lit up, 'I like going to the shops, and I like pretty dresses, can I have one?'

'Of course, let's go and tell Heather.' Then Angelika realised she should have asked Heather first. Fortunately, when they arrived, she looked much more cheerful.

'My bandage is coming off today, and that nice doctor came in and had a fascinating chat with me last night. And I enjoyed our discussion too, so, please, go and do some shopping. Might you get a few things for me? I have nothing to wear when I leave.'

Angelika scribbled down Heather's bra sizes and things like that, she even needed socks and shoes. Dulcie hadn't been in nightwear on the night of the storm, but when she was dressed, she looked older than her years in shabby trainers, t-shirt, and tracksuit bottoms. Angelika wondered why she hadn't noticed this before.

Outside the doors, Dulcie froze, her eyes were like saucers. 'I've never seen so many people!' She grabbed Angelika's hand and hung on to it as they caught a bus and made their way to a shopping centre. Angelika had revised her plans, Dulcie wouldn't cope with Oxford Street. She was silent, walking along, taking it all in, and at the Disney shop she stopped and looked at Angelika with blazing eyes.

'Go on then!'

Dulcie bolted in and ran from display to display, clearly wanting it all. She didn't grab anything; it looked like she was afraid to touch.

'It's ok, you can touch if you're gentle, but whatever we buy, we will pick it up on our way back, as we might lose it when we are shopping for other things. What is it you want?' Angelika saw that fleeting stubborn look, but Dulcie grabbed her hand and took her to the Frozen stand, she wanted both the princesses.

It was fun to give someone joy, so they took them to the counter and asked the assistant to keep them behind. Luckily, it was an understanding teenager who put them in a bag and hid it behind the counter with a grin. Angelika expected there might be some extra goodies inside on their return.

It wasn't all so easy. Dulcie didn't want to be measured for new bras and got totally coy when faced with buying packets of knickers. Sneakily, Angelika saw the bra size when Dulcie tried on a top, so she stealthily bought a couple. She found some chocolate and gave it to Dulcie to munch while she quickly filled Heather's shopping list.

Dulcie had no interest in the tops and trousers Angelika selected, her heart was clearly on her princess outfit. She wriggled and made excuses about her arm being in the way and hurting. Laden with bags, they made their way to Marks and Spencer.

Inside, Dulcie was in heaven, and to Angelika's surprise and delight, chose dresses with bright colours and only touches of glitter. She didn't really want to be a childish princess, but to have smart, attractive clothes. Then Angelika had to talk her out of wearing one of them on the bus back, as she would get cold. Dulcic grew tired and her arm clearly annoyed her.

Making their way to a café and feasting on chocolate cake and milkshakes got their energy levels up, and they made their way back to the Disney shop. The bag was bulging and Dulcie, in her joy, wouldn't carry anything else, leaving Angelika as the pack mule.

It was a relief to see the hospital doors. Dulcie revived enough to rush in and tell her mother all about the adventures, and Angelika had to help her into one of the dresses. At which point, after twirling around, Dulcie sat down in the comfortable chair and fell instantly asleep, with her unopened Disney bag at her side.

'I've never seen her so happy.' Heather sounded almost weepy. She looked quite different without the bandage and freshly washed hair.

'Do you hate me after our talk?'

'Of course not, what is done, is done. You have to talk to God about anything that worries you. He already knows all about it.' That got a glare in return.

'Here are your clothes.'

That brought the smile back as she tried everything on, even admiring the cheap trainers that fitted well.

'Perfect! Just the sort of things I like, but much smarter. We usually bought through catalogues. It was easier as we had to get a taxi everywhere. Are you taking Dulcie shopping again tomorrow? I don't know when I can pay you for all this, so I don't want to trespass on your kindness.'

'They're a present. I haven't told Dulcie anything about her being my sister. I thought I'd wait until you were both fit and well. We're going to London Zoo tomorrow, she's never seen tigers and lions. I hope she'll be strong enough for it.'

'Thank you so much, I'm truly in your debt. I'll work something out when I get home. Do you think the roof will be repaired soon?'

'I've no idea, I haven't spoken to anyone since we left.'

Heather seemed to be almost joyful, so they sat and chatted. Heather told her more about Dulcie's childhood, until, like Dulcie, she began to look tired.

Angelika left them to nap and made her way out. A text bleeped as she got on the bus. It was Glen asking her out for a meal, and Angelika laughed at herself for how happy that made her feel.

Stew was both happy and annoyed when Angelika got home. Brian and Sue had taken her up on to Clapham Common, where she had run amok, making friends with every dog she met, and chasing squirrels fruitlessly as they shot up into trees. It seemed she was telling Angelika about her day, and Angelika wished for those simpler times when all she thought of doing was taking a long walk along the beach.

Brian and Sue ribbed her about the date with mock warnings about Glen not being a Christian, but Sue lent Angelika some clothes, as she had only brought jeans and plain things with her. It was a pleasure to feel smart and get away from everyone, get some perspective on things. She already sensed that Glen was a good listener.

THE MEAL

He arrived on time and looked almost a stranger in a suit. His ginger hair had grown back so quickly. Again there was that sense of familiarity Angelika couldn't place. He grinned and rubbed his hand through it when he saw her gaze. 'Got a posh barber to cut all that brown out and be myself again. What have you been up to?'

As they drove through the early evening traffic, she told him the final revelations and twists in the tale.

'That's unbelievable. How are we all going to get through that one? Are you going to go back and tell them?'

'Can you imagine it? Possibly, the only way would be to put this all in writing and get that solicitor to tell them. All hell will break loose and I don't want to be the brunt of it, and certainly not on Dulcie. They are all equally guilty, but there is so much anger and resentment, only an act of God I think would break through all that.'

'Like a hand reaching through the clouds and given them all a good shake?'

'Oh, I wish he would!' Angelika laughed so hard, she snorted through her nose and had to use a handkerchief to wipe her face.

They were turning onto the forecourt of a smart hotel, and when they stopped, a valet came and took the keys.

'Wow, governor, this is a posh place for us innit?' Angelika couldn't resist saying.

'Now pipe down, Miss Angelika, they might

hear,' Glen responded in mock theatrical voice.

They grinned, remembering the same joke in an old sitcom.

'Your parents too?' Glen asked. For a split second Angelika saw her mother hunched over the TV watching the re-runs of her favourite sit-com, always wishing aloud she could live in the country. No, she wasn't ready to share that yet, so she smiled back at him and nodded.

Inside, they were whisked into an ultra modern bar, with uncomfortable stools, and low lighting. Glen gave her a stern look, so she just muttered, 'sorry sir' quietly.

Drinks were poured by a supercilious looking barman, but the cocktails tasted amazing.

'You may have to carry me home if I have more than one of these!' Angelika giggled.

'We can always book a room.'

Angelika mock glared at Glen, hopefully this wouldn't get spoilt by getting carnal. They were saved by a waiter saying their table was ready, so the moment passed unanswered.

The softly lit dining room was filled with furnishings reminiscent of the 1950s, with sleek furniture and candles. Angelika relaxed, as this was more to her taste. There was a retro menu of the 60s, 70s and every decade up to the present.

'Oh, this is amazing. My parents used to go on about their favourite meal, so I'm going 70s. Prawn cocktail, steak and chips, and black forest gateau,' Glen grinned. Angelika ordered the same, but turned down the Blue Nun wine for something more contemporary.

Over the meal, they kept off the present, and talked about anything else they could think of, finding much in common, except her faith, so they veered away from that. Glen seemed to Angelika to be someone she had always known, and at the same time, exciting. All these were new feelings for her, so she packed them to the back of her mind and stayed in the moment. All too soon, they were on the coffees and turning down bright green liqueurs.

'I'm back down to the coast in the next week or so. I want to see how the boat is and I might stay on it for a while. It's back in the water on the river as the yard is full of wrecked boats being mended. Would you like a lift back?' He truly was a gentleman.

'I'm not sure if I'm ready for all that fall out. How can I face them with what I know?' Angelika grimaced.

'I understand, it's a ticking bomb, can it be left ticking?'

'Or is there a bomb disposal expert to hand?' she grinned. 'I need to seek a way to deal with this. I will call that solicitor, there must be a way forward somehow. It can't go on as it did, but the change could be catastrophic. If Dulcie and Heather can't live in that house, where do they go? I'll call you, as I hope some solution will come to me.'

Too soon, they arrived back at Angelica's friends. After the usual, it was a wonderful evening stuff, then he swooped and kissed her full on the lips. With a gleeful grin, he leapt out of the car to open her door. She sat paralysed for a second, overwhelmed with something she'd never felt before.

On the kerb, she engulfed him in a hug that Dulcie would have been proud of and rushed indoors.

THE ZOO

Angelika felt a little like an obsessed teenager the next morning, no one had ever made her feel this way. It was like an awakening, something glowed inside her. She was almost her sixteen year old self, thoughts and emotions swirling around and making her a total muddle. It took an effort to keep her mind concentrated on the day ahead.

Dulcie and Heather waited for her in the dayroom, both in their new clothes, and there was a group hug which had Angelika's head spinning again. Such love.

'Now, Dulcie, you mind you take it easy with that arm, and if you get tired, say so.' Heather was in bossy mother mode, and she looked so much better. 'What time do you think you'll be back?' she asked.

'I've no idea, late afternoon, depending on buses. I don't think we'll go on the underground with all the pushing and shoving.'

'Great, have a fabulous day, and take some photos for me on your phone, Angelika?'

'Will do.'

Like a couple of school children, the pair set off on their adventure. Dulcie was far more relaxed on the bus now she was used to it and even asked to sit on the top floor.

At first in the zoo, she wanted to see it all in a rush, so Angelika made her stop and look at a large map on the wall and then decide what they would go and look at. The big cats came on top, so they spent an hour looking at tigers and lions, which shocked Dulcie at how big they were.

Sometimes her words of description failed her, and Angelika saw how frustrated she got when that happened, and so gave her new words. She learnt quickly, maybe this was how she had learnt so many hymns and praise songs when the church had a vicar.

After that they visited elephants, camels, then Angelika chose the zebras. After that, they sat for cake and drinks in a café, watching people go past. Then snakes and reptiles. In fact, by four o'clock, they had covered pretty well all the animals on the board, had eaten copious amounts of chips and ice cream, and were ready for home.

Angelika felt exhausted, it wasn't like going around the zoo with a mate, more like an overgrown ten-year-old. Dulcie still bounced around on all the sugar she had eaten as they raided the souvenir shop. The buses looked full as it was building for rush hour, so Angelika lashed out on a cab, which seemed to impress Dulcie even more than the zoo.

When they got back to the ward, a harassed nurse caught them and asked the pair to follow her to the nurses' station.

'Mrs Smith discharged herself this morning. She left us with a brief letter saying that as Dulcie's sister you would take her home and into your care. Is this correct?'

Angelika gasped for air, it was one thing doing trips out, but all day?

'What about her arm?'

'It will need re-ex raying in a few weeks, and then probably the plaster will come off. I've a letter here for her GP and the outpatient's department at Bridmouth hospital. This is too early for our liking, but we have a problem with bed blocking, as you know. I need you to sign these forms, too.'

Dulcie was fortunately checking out all the goodies she had bought and not listening.

'Her things are in these bags with the letters. There are also details of various support groups, NHS services and doctors in your home area which you might find helpful.' The nurse was trying her hardest to help.

What could Angelika do? 'Dulcie, we're going for another ride in a taxi!'

GOING HOME

'I am totally, utterly in your debt.'
Glen grinned with a touch of wickedness and gave her a wink.

'Don't worry, I've thought of how I'm going to get you to repay me!' Angelika knew she was blushing, but what could she do?

They were again cruising down the motorway in his car, the back seat of which was filled with an ecstatic Stew washing Dulcie while at the same time trying to grab the toy lion to tear into bits. The lion knew its days were numbered.

Dulcie had taken it with equanimity when told Heather had gone to stay with some friends and that they were going to Brian and Sue's with Angelika for a week or so before they might go back to their homes in Hamlet. She was having far too much fun to miss her mother.

Dulcie had instantly loved Brian and Sue and especially Stew, although at first she was a little rough with her. She quickly understood what the warning growl meant and learnt to respect the dog. Now they were the best of friends. Throwing balls for Stew in the common had her laughing hysterically with joy. The only problem Angelika saw was if Dulcie wanted to get some of her things from her home, which might be difficult if they had started work on it.

There was only one difficult but beautiful

incident in the past week. They were sitting in the middle of a packed bus. Dulcie turned to Angelika, and asked in a loud voice, 'Why aren't I like everyone else?'

Angelika was used to dealing with difficult situations, but this had her thrown for a while, so she asked, 'how do you mean?'

'Well, I have slanty eyes, and I stick my tongue out sometimes. My mother used to tap hers to remind me, but no one else does it.'

'You are like everyone else, Dulcie, because we are all different. God loves you for being you. Not everyone has slanty eyes, you are right, but not everyone has brown hair and green eyes like me. We are all a wonderful different.'

'And you don't have a big nose like me,' butted in a lady on the other seat.

'Or brown skin like me,' said another.

'And you can sing better than me, too,' added Angelika. This wasn't the best of responses as Dulcie broke into 'All things Bright and Beautiful', and many on the bus joined in.

Dulcie was making her first steps into the world she hadn't seen in her entire life and doing it with class. Yet again, Angelika had to repent from being annoyed with Heather for having denied her daughter a wider life.

On the first Sunday, Angelika took Dulcie to church with Brian and Sue. It wasn't one of the large, noisy auditorium ones, but after the church at Hamlet, everything would be big. It had live music and a straightforward service that wasn't too long. Dulcie was gobsmacked when she saw the filled seats, but she soon said hello and waved at everyone. She didn't know the words to all the songs, but joined in gustily, dancing away by her chair.

Dulcie found the sermon a little long and began to yawn, then jumped up and danced to the last song. She had no barriers and chatted to complete strangers, but she was in a safe place.

They were almost the last to leave. Hamlet would have to work hard to top this on a Sunday, but there were bigger churches in Bridmouth.

Yet now, travelling home, Angelika worried about what might happen when Dulcie needed her mother again. It had been the only option to take her home, London was only a place for treats.

What sort of reception they would receive was another concern, so Angelika sent a long WhatsApp to May, carefully explaining the situation, especially Heather's absence, but so far there had been no response.

That Heather could take off like that, leaving no contact details, was both understandable and infuriating. So much for her agoraphobia. Then in all fairness, it would be the first time she had some totally free time since Dulcie's birth. That must have been so tempting. But not to leave an address or switch her phone on? The only consolation was that she would guess where Angelika would take Dulcie and turn up.

Angelika had been looking forward to seeing more of Glen to explore her fledgling relationship, not to be lumbered full time with a brand new sister, and couldn't help but feel a little irked. Teenager again. He had taken it with surprising good humour and immediately offered to drive them home as he was going that way again, anyway.

As they drove down the busy roads, he hummed to the radio, which Angelika heard between talking to the two in the back. It annoyed her that she still couldn't place why the humming seemed so familiar.

All too soon, they hit the outskirts of Bridmouth and stopped at a supermarket to get supplies. Angelika had no idea what Dulcie liked to eat, so she dragged her away from the dog and made her push the trolley. It seemed like Dulcie would live on baked beans and mashed potato, so she put them and a selection of things she knew kids liked in the trolley and hoped for the best.

'You know, I'm quite apprehensive at what our reception will be,' Angelika said quietly to Glen.

'They will have had time to calm down, and you threw that thing about money at them all, that should go a long way. Did you mean it?' Glen asked with a smile.

'Yes, and while talking to Heather, I thought of another way of using it. After all those years of paying to support those two, everyone must have given a lot of money. I could twist my idea of a gift. Split the money between them according to how much they had given, and then it would be like a repayment. It would put Heather in the clear, although deep down, I think they should sort this out face to face. Then this would take the sting out of the revelation of her deception. But if they had decided on the terms I left them with, they might be angry when they were changed.'

'And if she never returns, do they even need to know?'

Angelika glanced on to the back seat to where Dulcie was asleep, she had a huge capacity for it. The lion was disembowelled.

'I'm sort of hoping that she's gone to find her family, it sounded like she had a large one. Then perhaps the maternal strings will bring her back to Dulcie.'

'And if not?'

'I'd never put her in a home, she's my sister, but she really should mix with her peers. There would be a way, I'm sure.'

'Do you feel lumbered?' Glen unconsciously echoed her worries.

'Never,' answered Angelika fiercely, a little driven by guilt at her earlier feelings, had he seen this? He didn't reply, and she began to think that this baby love between them had been snuffed out. Yet, who would blame him, who would want a partner with a large child in tow? Sadness and tiredness engulfed her.

HAMLET

Rattling over the cattle grid brought mixed emotions of happiness at being home and dread of any further arguments.

They stopped outside Beau house as Angelika now knew it was named. Little had changed, the bright blue tarp was still on the roof. Angelika gently woke Dulcie, and they went inside to collect a few of her things. In her belongings, they had found the front door key. Although Angelika had no memory of locking the door when they left, they found it locked. Who else had a key?

The house was dark and stank of damp. There was no electricity, so the pair of them scuttled upstairs and collected bits and pieces to the torch on Angelika's phone. Dulcie cringed as they passed the kitchen. Angelika was always one for facing things, so opened the door. To her surprise, someone had cleaned.

'Dulcie, look. It's all clean now. Like when God forgives you, after you've said sorry in your prayers. There is no more fight between you and your mother, it's all healed.'

Dulcie looked a little weepy, but nodded, then got out of the house as quickly as she could. Angelika followed, still wondering who had cleaned up?

There must have been rain, as there was no dust as they drove down. Angelika had fleeting glances of Teresa's garden, all brown and ruined. The church seemed to be untouched, although the oak that stood behind it was leaning at a precarious angle on the roof.

Scaffolding and more blue tarpaulin engulfed several of the houses where chimneys were being rebuilt. In front of them, the sea bank no longer dipped in the middle, it was all the same height, even if the mend was uncovered with grass.

The surrounding fields looked an odd sort of green, so the salt must have done some damage. There were no cattle in sight, just the children's ponies eating from a hayfeeder in their field. This wasn't good.

Her own house seemed to have been the least affected of them all, should she have offered it for people to stay in, instead of disappearing? Too late now. Hamlet was deserted, there were no visitors outside the café, especially since all the benches had swum away.

The four of them made their way up the path and staggered in to drop their bags in the kitchen. No one had been in to clean here. The kettle was soon on the boil and they sat around the table, dunking biscuits in their mugs of tea.

'What will you do now, Glen?' Angelika hoped he wouldn't bolt off.

'I'm going to have another check of my cottage, now things have calmed down. Take some photos and see if it is repairable. I do have a soft spot for it.'

'The boat will be cramped after London, you're always welcome here.' Was she really that desperate for him not to go?

'I know that.' His grin made her slightly less worried about things. 'I'm going to shoot off now. Will you keep me in the loop about things? If there's a flare up before you meet up with them tomorrow, I'm not far away and I think you'll need someone on your side if they do.'

She blushed her thankfulness. Glen leant over and kissed her on the cheek, then got up and reached to give Dulcie a kiss too, which she ducked, obviously shy and embarrassed. They exchanged huge grins over her head and he left with a wave, humming that tune again. Mentally shaking herself, Angelika got into action.

'Let's make your bed up and you can bring all your things up there and set them out. There's a chest of drawers in the next room, which I'll get for you.'

Dulcie was thrilled with her new bed and bounced on it as Angelika went into the other room. It brought back a chill, seeing all the dead people's things as she emptied underwear into a bag out of the drawers. She would have to deal with this, Dulcie needed better than the box room.

Once the room was in order, they took Stew into the garden and there got a huge surprise. The family of ducks were swimming around on the pond, but someone must have been in with a digger, as it was now much bigger and lined with black plastic. Bits of loose weed from the original pond floated around.

Angelika was in someone's good books. Or was it due to you saying you would help financially said the cynical voice at the back of her head? The male duck came up and quacked at her as if saying something, the others were still dabbling at the edge.

'I think he's saying he likes the fresh water,' Dulcie said.

'Wow, Dulcie, you speak duck! And you're right, if there is salt in the ground, it will make the water taste horrible to them. Shall we get them some food?'

The feed bin was half empty, so someone knew about her ducks and cared. Angelika couldn't stop herself welling up. I'm just overtired, she thought. But it made her feel so much easier about returning. The ducks were soon tucking in.

Really, they should take Stew for a walk, she'd neglected her so much lately. But Stew was already back in the house, and had helped herself to a stuffed elephant, much to Dulcie's laughter. It was the first time Angelika heard Dulcie do a belly laugh, and she thanked God for her new, wonderful family that she had never expected to have.

They were both tired and after watching Dulcie's favourite soap; it was an early night for everyone.

THE NEXT DAY

Angelika awoke with the sunlight on her face, aware that Stew lay on the bed, but had grown. On turning over, she found Dulcie next to her, snoring louder than the dog.

Fair enough, she might have been too scared to do this in London, but they would have to make some rules about this. Angelika savoured the semi quiet moment with the sound of the waves in the distance.

There was a better view of the sea now the trees were bare. What an idyll, if only she didn't have to face everyone in Hamlet after the rushed departure. She spent some time thanking, praising and asking God what on earth he had in mind for her in the next couple of days. All she got as a reply was that sense of wonderful peace in her spirit, which even relieved some of the raging teenage emotions that had returned after all those years. Angelika forgot her worries and set about waking the sleeping beauties.

In this quiet time, Angelika took a deep breath and told Dulcie in very short simple sentences about the death of Veronica's baby and how she had been born shortly after. That she was Heather's daughter, and so her name wasn't Hutton.

'I know that. Mother told me ages ago. We decided I would be lady Hutton in memory of the baby. A lady is like a princess, Mother said, so I am happy with this name. Why are names important anyway?' Dulcie was puzzled.

'They're not important at all, you can be who you want to be.' So why had Heather insisted Dulcie hadn't been told? Was she actually getting gaga? What did it matter? Dulcie knew exactly who she was, which was the most important thing. Angelika dropped the subject.

Breakfast was no longer a quiet way into the day, but a confusion of finding dog food, toast, eggs and Dulcie's favourite cereal, which had vanished. Into all this walked May, with that same loving look as on the day Angelika arrived, and with an equally large coffee cake.

'Mines with two sugars,' she grinned. 'Dulcie, come and give us a hug, I haven't seen you for years!' She asked for that, thought Angelika as May came out of the sumo hold.

'Phew, I'd forgotten those,' she said, sitting down promptly on a stool. 'It's great to have you back again.'

'Really? After the storm and it's repercussions?' asked Angelika.

'Absolutely. We've all had time to calm down, catch up on our sleep, reflect, forgive and learn.'

That was pretty deep for May.

'I'm so glad, I didn't want not to be friends with everyone.' May now got a relieved hug from

Angelika. 'We have a lot of things to discuss, can we meet up at the café sometime soon? Is the chimney repaired? How are the dogs?'

'Of course, tonight? Yes, and fine!' May laughed. 'There may still be things that aren't quite sorted out, but they are minor issues that we won't come to blows on, I'm sure.'

It wasn't totally hunky dory then; they weren't going to like a lot of her news either. She felt the power inside her, wanting reconciliation and truth, for in it lay her peace. So be it.

'Who did the pond? The ducks are thrilled.'

'Ron did that, they had to reline the drinking pond for the cattle and there was enough leftover to do yours and the one at the top of the lane.'

Why couldn't May say Beau house?

'I must thank him tonight. Is the sea wall fixed?' Angelika kept on smiling.

'As far as possible without concrete defences and we don't want that, it would bring too many people down here.'

But they wouldn't need to be so secretive in the future. Tonight was going to be a changing of the ways. Aware she was away with the fairies; Angelika grabbed a knife and served the cake for breakfast to a thrilled Dulcie.

'I couldn't find her cereal, although we bought some!' Angelika laughed off the situation.

'How's Glen?' asked May.

'Fine. He's on his boat, which is back in the water as the yard is full of repairs. He'll be along some time this evening.'

'Did you see much of him in London?'

'Yes, they went to eat in the restaurant and didn't take me!' spluttered Dulcie through a mouthful of cake.

'When you have a boyfriend, you won't want Angelika with you!' retorted May, much to everyone's surprise. Dulcie hid her head and ate more cake. The two women grinned conspiratorially.

'Now, don't eat too much, Dulcie, we've a party tonight, and you'll need a nice dress,' May ordered. Was this how people had treated Dulcie even though she was a grown woman? Angelika sensed her hackles rising, but there would be time to address this.

'Shall we bring anything?'

'Pizzas?'

'We'll get some,' Angelika grinned at Dulcie, 'we enjoy shopping. First though, we're going for a good walk, to get rid of all that London air.'

Watching Dulcie and Stew playing on the beach was the most simple of joys. It didn't matter that Dulcie couldn't throw straight, or that Stew often ignored the throw anyway when there was something delightful to sniff. All three of them kicked in the shallowest waves and came home a little damp around the edges.

Pizzas bought, the early afternoon had them taking baths and putting on smart clothes.

'Now, you're sure, Dulcie, that you are ready

for this? There might be shouting and bad things said about your mother. It's because people are hearing news that they don't like. This is your home, and we're going to make it happy again like when you were little. You will be brave?'

She nodded to all of this, for Brian, Sue and Angelika had carefully explained that her mother had made mistakes, and people might still be unhappy about this. Dulcie had her serious face on and was clearly deep in thought as she now asked some questions about where her mother was. All Angelika could say was that she had gone to visit where she used to live. The stage was set.

THE MEETING

The three of them set off in the twilight, and entering the café was like going into a familiar haven. Yet, for the first time, Angelika saw that the room looked tired, the books dusty and worn; the furniture needing a good clean. Had it been like this before, or was it just her new perspective on things?

Ted came from the back to take the warm pizzas with the dogs following him close behind, and Dulcie had a blissful time being washed by them. Angelika smiled as she saw Dulcie was being careful to keep her clothes clean.

As people arrived, they all seemed pleased to see them, and there was an essence of the original peace that Angelika had found when she first arrived. At least they weren't all queuing up to ask her to do things any more. Glen had warned her he would be late, something to do with tides. She missed his quiet energy, but she had that spiritual inner strength tonight that would carry her through this ordeal.

Dulcie became steadily more shy with the large number of people, and sat close to Angelika. The food was devoured, and the children went off to watch TV in the back room. They asked Dulcie to go with them, but she remained stubbornly shy.

As the coffee went round, Roy stood up, and Angelika suddenly realised the mitigating presence of Henry wasn't there.

'Henry has just rung me; he's running late as he's just finishing some plastering and he wants the whole wall done in one go. He asked me to keep some order here and leave some whisky for him.' Everyone sniggered politely.

'It's great to see Angelika and, er, Dulcie here. I understand that they have things they want to tell us, and we have things for them!' He tried a smile. 'Angelika, would you like to start?'

She refused to get up and talk like in an office meeting. Everyone would simply have to make an effort to hear. She took Dulcie's hand under the table.

'When I came here, I felt loved and accepted, but that there was a deep secret behind this lovely community.' Good soft soaping there.

'Over time, I heard about how the commune began, due to a legacy left by Veronica Hutton, who died in childbirth. That you all pulled together and looked after her daughter, Dulcie. You paid for her and her carer, Heather, over the decades.'

'Since then, in an attempt to keep secret how you had come upon your houses, which was based on pieces of paper with a few scribbled drunken words on them.' She guessed here, but by the looks on some faces, she had hit home.

'I learnt also that over the years, this relationship deteriorated as you grew older and generations lay further away from the truth. That Heather, in the past couple of years, has become steadily more difficult. But still you didn't make any effort to help them, leaving them steadily more isolated and sad. Well, shame on you all. Not one of you had the guts to even go to a solicitor and sort things out. Hadn't you even thought of squatter's rights, which comes in after twenty-five years, I believe?'

'But we had it in writing, that was different,' Ted almost shouted.

'You could have torn those bits of paper up at anytime,' Angelika retorted, reacting to the rising annoyance. 'Now please, I'm trying not to anger you, there is a solution,' she continued in what she hoped was a calming voice.

Things quietened.

'After the storm, I told you about the inheritance I didn't need that would pay for all your costs, and I was more than happy to do this. Shortly afterwards, I found Dulcie and Heather injured and none of you had done a thing to help them. Shame on you again.' In a split second, she saw a purely sour look on May's face, and that was a shock. Angelika ploughed on.

'I followed them to London and finally heard Heather's side of the story. Of how she's been trapped here for ages, and couldn't find a way out. Of her unhappy life before she came here, which none of you took time to find out about. Yes, she says there were lovely years here as the first generation grew, many of you were friends with Dulcie, but as you moved towards adulthood and married life, she didn't. You left her behind. Shame on you all again.'

'Then Heather told me a hidden part of this story and it's possible that the joke may have been on you lot all along. Veronica's daughter died shortly after birth. Of course, you were all too stoned to notice. Dulcie is Heather's daughter.'

There was a complete uproar with people shouting, blaming each other and acting like folk who've been duped. Angelika took a wine bottle and banged it on the table. She glanced down at Dulcie who was eating a pizza and handing bits to Stew. Clever girl.

'Hey, listen to me!' They quietened. 'I don't know if anyone has kept accounts over the years, of how much each of you has paid. My offer is this to you. Take all of my money, and I've yet to work out how much that is, along with all my inheritance from Phil. Put this under a financial manager and use this to finish all the repairs and have some repayment for your outgoings for all the years that you have supported them.'

'YOU'RE GOING TO DO WHAT WITH MY MONEY?' roared a voice from the back of the room, no one had heard the door opening. There stood two dead people, wearing loud Hawaiian shirts and bronzed tans. The room fell silent except for Dulcie and Stew chewing noisily on pizza crusts.

PANDEMONIUM

'I haven't even met my daughter yet, and she's selling the family jewels. Good on you, kid, they've needed someone to take them to task for years.' Phil strode into the room, swept Angelika up from the bench and engulfed her in a first ever real father hug. If the room had been in an uproar before, this was a riot. All shouted and yelled their views, saying they wanted the money, some not, others asking where the flipping heck the two had been all of this time.

Angelika looked down at Dulcie, who now had her hands over her ears. She began to scream. A primeval, nerve annoying, nails on the chalkboard sound that tore through everything going on around her. She didn't stop until everyone shut up and sat down. She closed her mouth and stood up.

Then, in her calm and husky voice, which she didn't rise, she made possibly the longest speech she had ever made in her life.

'You all don't like my mother, and she didn't like you. It serves you right for being mean to her. My mother knows she has been naughty and has said sorry to Jesus for it. But Jesus loves you, and you should live like him, not like a lot of naughty pigs. Angelika is my lovely sister, and she loves

Jesus, too. You should be happy like us and forgive people. Like Gerard used to say in church, which none of you came to. We had lovely services, and we sang lovely songs, but not one of you came. Silly people.'

In the silence, she sat down and picked up some more pizza. Hadn't she eaten enough yet, Angelika wondered? Now there was murmuring, no one took control of speaking. Phil and Mary grabbed seats and sat down next to Angelika.

'I have two daughters?'

Angelika grinned at a face that she hadn't known all her life until now and should have done. The one man who had been kind to her mum, even though he had gone too. He had a thick beard and bushy grey eyebrows, but he was instantly familiar. There was so much and nothing to say.

Before she formed a word, a cold draught came into the room, and three more people came in. This is like something from one of those bad Hallmark films, Angelika thought when she saw who it was.

Henry spoke first, without raising his voice. 'Dulcie's right you know. You can all stop being angry and mean, and begin to love again, we have money for all. When I was plastering tonight, I smashed through a void in the wall in Gerard's side of the house. Ladies and gentlemen, I present you with Gerard's stash!' In his hands, he lifted two bags clearly stuffed full with rolls of banknotes.

'We always thought he was dealing as well as

growing the stuff but never proved it, especially when he found Jesus and took over the church. We all searched that many times, didn't we?' he grinned at everyone.

In the hubbub, Angelika felt a nudge at her side, Dulcie wanted to whisper something. 'Gerard was the funny man at the church, he taught me to sing. It made me sad when he died.'

So there never had been a vicar, just one of the commune, when would all these revelations finish? Dulcie suddenly rushed off her chair and hurtled towards the door where Heather stood there looking awkward with who? Good grief, it was the bone doctor.

Sensing the rush of antagonism in the room, Angelika's head began to spin. Heather was engulfed in a sumo hug and gave one back, so Angelika stood up as Phil said something to Mary and walked over to the doctor, who was looking forlorn. She shook hands with him as he seemed that sort of man.

'I have some things to tell these people on this night of revelation, do you think they will let me?' he asked in a surprisingly quiet voice.

'I'll get their attention!' Angelika put her fingers in her mouth and made the ear-piercing whistle she had learnt while working on a sheep farm. That did the trick.

'I'm frightfully sorry to interrupt, but I have some more news for you. My name is Dr Terry Evans, and I met Heather when she was in a hospital in London. For years, since I left university, I have researched the Hutton family.'

Everyone in the room stiffened.

'The family line died out with Veronica, you need have no fears about that. It is the earlier history you need to be concerned with. Back in the reign of Charles the second, this land was a highly profitable salterns or saltings. When he came to the throne, he rented this land to the Huttons for a peppercorn rent, in thanks for all they had done for him in his exile.'

'When the railways came and salt was imported, the industry died. The Huttons kept the land and never bought it. The monarchy forgotten all about it. Veronica never had the right to give you your homes, all of this land belongs to the King.'

This time there was silence, as everyone was overloaded with information from all directions. Terry ploughed on. 'It's possible that you can claim the land or ask the Crown estate if you can buy it as it's possibly what's known as 'Escheat' land. Heather and I have spent some wonderful days going through all the family documents in the boxes and trunks which were left in what was the loft of her house. There is so much information in there that I am retiring to become a full-time historian and fight your cause for the land.'

He stood back expecting a cheer, but everyone was just too drained, except for one faint hip hooray from somewhere in the back.

Angelika felt a hand on her shoulder and saw Glen looking down at her. He took her hand, and they sneaked away from the ensuing discussion, which they heard later continued until milking time. They walked in the light of a full moon down to the sea bank and sat together, ignoring the damp ground.

'The plot gets thicker and thicker,' sighed

Glen and put his arm around her. Angelika wanted to stay forever in this wonderful, comforting place in his arms, but the revelations had her head spinning. All her teenage adventures were nothing compared to this warm joy, but her peace had gone.

'I have a father. I can't believe this. It's too much to process, after a lifetime of being an orphan,' she finally managed to say.

'It's a good thing though, surely?'

'Of course, but I don't know how to deal with all this.'

Everything welled up inside her, and for the first time in decades, she cried. Tears of happiness, confusion, and pain. Glen hugged her, let her be, and then gave her a slightly grotty handkerchief.

'Better now? I think you need some space to think this through and maybe, for once, as I know you mean the best, let them sort themselves out. Staying out of all this will mean you won't feel responsible for them, and you're not. Go home and sleep, you must be exhausted after all of this, even the time with Dulcie must have taken its toll despite the fun it was.'

He was right, and she agreed with him, but she didn't want him to go.

'I know, I can't help feeling responsible for them. Maybe after a good night's sleep, I'll get my head together.'

He hugged her closer. 'I have to go back to London yet again, I'm appointing someone to run my new business for me, so I don't have to be going back and forth all the time. There are much more important things to deal with.'

He stood, and taking her hand, walked her home. Angelika didn't want to ask what the important things were, in case they didn't involve her. Instead, they talked about the moon and Glen told her a long, rambling story about a sailing trip in Spain. She detected that he wasn't wanting to discuss things further, either.

At the door, he gave her another courteous kiss, and left with a firm, 'Let them sort themselves out!'

A TALK WITH FATHER

'We need to have a chat, don't we?' Phil looked blearily at Angelika. They were all sitting in the kitchen, which was full of bits and pieces of luggage. Her parents had got back from the party and it was about 3 am. Stew had woken Angelika, barking at the intruders. Dulcie came in first, looking exhausted and had gone straight to bed, saying her mother had gone with the silly doctor to a hotel and hadn't taken her, but she didn't seem truly annoyed.

Now, Dulcie was snoring upstairs, and Angelika had just been letting Stew out. Her parents were home! That made her smile as she said it to herself.

Phil, with an annoyed expression on his face, suddenly demanded, 'What the dickens have you done with MY house and MY money?' Mary tried to intervene by grabbing his arm to get attention, but he shrugged it off, even when she shouted, 'it was never your house Phil, don't forget that it's mine.'

All the strain of the evening welled up inside Angelika. 'This is not your house, you are dead and whatever identity you have now, you don't own it either. Nor does Mary, nor do I. All your money is untouched in the bank account, but it's not your name, is it?' Angelika exploded. To her surprise, he shrank back and sat down on the chair, speechless. Had no one spoken to him like that before?

'Sorry love.' Mary, who was short, plump and a complete mother figure with short grey hair, smiled at her. 'It's all been a bit of a shock to him, and he had too much to drink. I think he somehow thought he would swan back here, everyone would laugh and he could pick up where he left off. I'll get him to bed, but can you help me move some more things out of the bedroom so I can make up the bed?'

Hence the contrite figure, with two mugs of coffee in his hands, who was making his way out the big windows to the sunny spot in the garden. They sank down into the chairs in silence, neither one knowing how to start. Mary, who had known Dulcie in her childhood, had taken her and Stew for a walk up the lane, they were going to fetch some of Dulcie's toys from the house.

On the way, Mary would tell Dulcie the truth about her father. Mary was everything that Angelica had ever wanted in a mother. She'd sensed the love radiating out from her in the short conversation they'd had before the other two woke up. It had taken every fibre of Angelika's body not to throw herself into the maternal arms. That Mary, who had been a childless widow before she met Phil, could still radiate love, must mean that she had God's hands on her.

'How did you meet my mum?' Angelika asked Phil, knowing she sounded belligerent, but it served him right.

He took a huge gulp of coffee and Angelika wondered if there was whisky in it for dutch courage.

'I was on shore leave in Pompey and met her in that club near the old town. No special story, we ended up at her place, and I bombed out there until my ship left port. She was a nice kid. For a while we had a great time, and I left her with new clothes and things in the flat and some money. If only I had stayed…oh, I lie. Ships in the night.'

'I will say in my defence that I came back on my next leave about a year later, but she had disappeared. Neighbours said she'd had a kid, so I wasn't going to search hard for her in case it was mine. I spent many years travelling the world, getting into all sorts of scrapes, but I never forgot her.' He winced as he saw the stony look on Angelika's face.

'It was only when I settled down here with Mary and I had some time to reflect that I thought I'd try to find her. Mary's into ancestry and so, as I had a maiden name, your mum wasn't difficult to find, and then you. Then we went on our trip where the car fell over the cliff and I talked Mary into a new life.'

'Who are you now?'

'Phil Chivers, Mr and Mrs Chivers. We were in Singapore when we read about the storm, and I had to come back, because I like this marshy old piece of England. I've been all over the world in my life, this is the only place I've settled in, maybe I'm finally getting old.'

He sounded contrite, but Angelika wasn't convinced. 'I wonder how many children you might have around the world? I might have many brothers and sisters and you know personally of one more, very close to here.'

Phil turned as white as a sheet. 'I thought it was Heather, when I saw her just after I married Mary, but I managed to talk myself out of it. When I learnt she was looking after a kid for someone and had done for years, I put things out of my mind. I never dreamed it was mine.'

'IT? Didn't you even ask about HER at the time? You blanked Heather, almost setting her on a breakdown. She only wanted an acknowledgment.'

Oh, at last, that was a genuinely shamefaced look.

'Your eldest daughter is Dulcie,' Angelika continued, 'and she's a better person than you will ever be. Don't you ever dare look at her as anything but a complete human. If I find you patronising her, or treating her as a child, I will do everything I can possibly do to stop you from getting your hands on this place. Do you understand?'

He nodded.

'Right, now we've got all that out of the way, let's start again. What do you want to know about me?' Angelika smiled, and Phil looked even more scared than before.

She saw this had never entered his head, and he searched for words. Angelika let him stumble about. She enjoyed every second of his pain, then took pity on him, she couldn't let her life be filled with unforgiveness. He was her father, and they had to begin somewhere. She smiled and told him a blunt version of her life, school, running away, the Salvation Army, the years working in job after job, serving God and never finding a home.

Phil took all she said with a calm disinterest, which made her want to go on trying to ram it into him, to make him have some feeling for his daughter. Then she saw a tear trickle down his cheek. She stood, grabbed his hand, and pulled him to his feet. 'Dad. Do you know, I've never been able to say that to anyone except God? But you're here now and we have something precious that I never thought to find. Let's be mates?'

They were both snottily snuffling by then and were surprised to find a large hanky being shoved between them.

'He's my dad too, you know?'

FAMILY

A day was spent with much discussion, healing and growing. Dulcie was ever angling to get Phil to meet with Heather. This was the one stumbling block as she now fixated that her mother and Phil should now marry. Mary once again showed Dulcie her wedding ring and the wedding photos, then finally, she accepted it with sadness.

Phil, now forgiven, told them more about his life and Mary filled in on the bits that he left out, such as his disastrous marketing ideas and the boat. When Angelika asked why there were no photos, he went to the largest picture in the hall, took it down and revealed a safe.

From inside he pulled out photos of himself over the years, and these told stories he hadn't said. Of a life at sea and getting up to no good, which was why he hid any photos of himself. Perhaps Mary was now his safe, forever haven. From this, Dulcie insisted they took photos of her new family on Angelika's phone. When they looked at them, the family likeness shone out. There was no doubt at all they were kin.

In the afternoon there came a knock at the door which set Stew barking at the top of her voice, she seemed to read the knocks. In came Mr Stephens, carrying with him more revelations.

He was soon sitting at the kitchen table with a large mug of tea, which Mary seemed to have constantly on the brew. They all sat waiting for his news. What else might emerge from the past?

'Thank you for contacting me, Angelika. I think I've got notes on all the matters you raised. As you know Phil, you are legally dead and your estate has passed to your daughter.'

'Don't I get any?' demanded Dulcie.

Steven looked at her and grinned. 'Hang on, sweetheart, we'll get this sorted!' Dulcie turned bright red and was coy for the rest of the time he was there. Phil, Mary, and Angelika tried not to laugh.

'Now, do you want to resurrect Phil King?' Steven asked.

'No.' Phil looked ashamed.

'Well, in that case, all these things will have to be dealt with and signed for by your daughter. I don't want to know anything about how you fixed this, I really don't.'

Phil clearly didn't like that, but he was stuffed.

Mary piped up. 'Steven, one thing I want you to know is that I emailed your father just after the car accident. I wanted him to know what Phil had done and try to stop it. Sorry, love, but it was a daft thing to do, and now you have little money left.' Phil looked away. Angelika wondered if he had more hidden money somewhere. He'd talked about gambling and dodgy, lucrative deals.

Steven cleared his throat. 'There were no records of that, but many files had disappeared when he retired. He got, well, a little eccentric. There's nothing left we can do, you'll have to work your non death out between yourselves and I. Do. Not. Want. To. Know. OK? Also, Angelika, my apologies if I seemed offhand when we first met, we were deep in sorting out Father's mess and I was worried he had done something disastrous.'

They nodded.

'Dulcie, I understand you are now registered with the NHS, but have no birth certificate. It is also an offence not to register a death, i.e. that of Veronica and her daughter.' Dulcie smiled with a red face.

'Can't we just let them go? The baby didn't have a birth or even a death certificate either,' interjected Angelika.

'I'm going to have to look into this. The Hutton family has died out, but there may still be legal documents to do with the estate that I will need to read. Terry has been in touch with me, and we'll go through all he has found. Likewise, the gift of the estate to the original commune. I can't believe how utterly stupid they have all been for so many years. If they had done something at the time, it could all have been easily resolved.'

'I will work with Terry and the Crown estate to see if we can find any early documentation. All this may involve fines and court cases. Thank you, your fees are going to help my business expand into a whole new territory.'

YET ANOTHER SESSION
AT THE CAFÉ

A couple of weeks later, Angelika rang round everyone to arrange a meeting at the café after she had squared it with May. Each phone call had been met with some echo of hostility, but when she said everything was going to be sorted out, friendliness was in the goodbyes.

Everyone turned out, and the room buzzed as Angelika stood up to talk to everyone. All except Glen, who still hadn't returned. ▓▓▓. She was astonished at this all-consuming need to see him again. Noone had ever made her feel like that.

The room shushed as Steven came in, and if anything, it went quieter still as he explained all the legal processes that would be needed to own Hamlet and sort out the births and deaths. It was more complicated, but more possible than he had thought.

'Now, I urge you, do the right thing and stop all these lies that have dogged you for years.' He sat down with a plop, looking exhausted.

Henry stood up. 'We have been talking too, and we will go through all these things you suggest. It will be good to stop skulking about, looking over our shoulders all the time. Everything will come out of Gerard's stash and there will be money left to pay us back for caring for Heather and Dulcie over the years.' He glared towards Honey and Poppy, who were probably still on about those new cars.

Phil now stood up, and clearly hadn't listened properly, but nobody passed comment. 'I will pay for anything else. For the first time in my life, I feel a fool. You all know what I did, and yes, Steven has agreed to sort out some, er, legal matters for me. As I'm now a father, perhaps I actually need to grow up at last.' Everyone cheered, although someone at the back, in a muffled voice, said, 'thank heavens for no more racing pigeons.'

Then Terry stood up. Angelika began to wonder if this was going to turn into a committee meeting with a hammer and gavel.

'This morning, Heather agreed to come and help me with my research and we will write a definitive book on the Hutton family!'

There came a subdued cheer, it seemed Heather had to do some work at reconciliation with people.

Terry continued. 'This joy was then overblown by my first trip into the graveyard to see all the Hutton burials. Have none of you been there since the flood? I can see not. The three shallow graves were washed out by the water, but as the graveyard has a wall, the bones are now all in a heap by the far corner. I've had a close look, and found the evidence that Veronica was indeed the last Hutton, in the shape of her digits, this is formed when...' there came a cough and a shove from Heather. 'Sorry, too much information. Enough to say, I can sort the bones out and I suggest in the name of decency, they now have a proper burial with all the rites.'

Another voice butted in. 'Yes, Gerard might have been a total headcase pothead, but in his last years, when he found his faith, he got off the drugs. He helped Dulcie, and it was a shame none of you attended his services, they were simple and sweet.' Mary, who had spoken, looked tearful. Dulcie, who was next to her, took her hand and smiled. Phil looked suspiciously at Mary out of the corner of his eye, so she shoved him in the ribs with everyone looking.

'I can take the service, but I'll need to buy some vestments,' Angelika offered. From then, things took a jollier turn. Dulcie caught Angelika when they were getting a drink.

'Angelika, I don't understand. Mother is making a book with Terry. What does that mean? Is she not my mother anymore? My father is Phil, but he's married to Mary and has another name. You are my half sister, what is that? Is Mary my Mum now too? I'm grown up, do I need two mothers? Do I have a real family now, it doesn't seem right. I can't understand it all, it's too much for me.' It was clear that all the times they had talked to her over the past weeks hadn't been understood.

The pair of them went outside and sat on a bench by the front door. Angelika explained how it all worked, even drew pictures and lines on the back of an old cigarette packet they found on the ground.

'So, I have a huge family. Who do I live with forever?'

This was the centre of Dulcie's problem.

'All of us, for as little or as long as you want. With me, we can go to zoos and church together.'

'And shopping?'

'Most definitely shopping!' They grinned at each other.

'You can live with Heather when you want, or you can live with Phil and Mary when you want. Or you can live in a flat or house on your own, with someone to help with the cooking,' Angelika grinned.

Dulcie laughed at this, she had tried to make breakfast for Phil and Mary one morning and had nearly burnt the house down.

'I'm happy now. I don't need to be on my own all the time, I have lots of family. I can be with family and be myself,' she said, tears running down her face.

Angelika hugged her, and they sat for a while until she mopped the tears up.

'Shall we go back to the party?'

'Dulcie nodded and rushed back into the cafe.

Angelika was about to follow when she heard

someone humming that familiar tune behind her. Spinning around, she saw Glen coming along the track, and in the distance, his boat was moored close to the shore.

In that split second, it all came back to her, and she ground to a halt. Finally, that song had words. Perhaps it was all that talk and memories of family recently that had put the piece of the puzzle into place.

There had been one lad who was different in her school group. A shy lad on the fringe of her gang. He didn't look like others, still wearing ordinary pullovers and jeans, not the crazy stuff they found to wear. His hair was short too, and not gelled. Somehow, he had become part of her group. Angelika discovered his wicked sense of humour, whether it was schoolboy stuff, it didn't matter, he'd made her laugh, which was a rare thing.

That morning he put dry ice in her hot chocolate, giving her a foaming cup like from a horror movie. Then one evening, when they were all sitting in the pub, she found he could sing. He sang one of the group faves from the past in a light tenor voice. She admired him like no other lad she met, but didn't really understand why. His shyness kept him out of the immoral core of the group and brought him a lot of jokes from the other lads, but he had an answer for them all. This admiration was an unknown thing for her, something never factored into her relationships before or since.

But school was soon over, and they went

their different ways, and Angelika had firmly battened down all her memories, closing down her past. Now the door was re-opened with a surge of joy.

'Harry, why didn't you tell me you were you?' She shrieked and rushed to him, grabbed his shoulders and held him at arms' length.

He stopped for a moment, relief and joy flashed across his face, and then he grinned. 'I wanted to see if we could love each other for ourselves, now, not based on years ago. If there had been a real, special attraction, it would work now, too. When it became clear you didn't remember me, even when I hummed Mr Blue Sky, I thought the past didn't matter after all. Then I changed my mind and wanted you to remember us as we were in that friendship we had back then. Am I daft? I wanted it all ways.'

'I changed my name for the last company launch as they thought Harry was not hip enough. This lot here never noticed the difference.'

'Oh, you were so clever. I can understand all that. We pick up at how we left off, but without teenage angst! Didn't you ever want to tell me?' Angelika smiled.

'Many, oh, so many times!'

They walked to the beach and sat down in the bank's lee again, sheltered from the cold wind.

'Those days were fun; I can still see that mug of dry ice.' Angelika snuggled into his arms.

'Anything, it was anything to get your

attention,' he chuckled.

'I don't think you would have liked it so much when you got it. I was pretty fickle then.'

'Oh, I knew about that. I hoped that one day you would run out of lads to chase and see me, but it never happened. I felt we had some connection that was beyond that.'

'And I was so messed up, I couldn't see it. Have you really waited all these years for me?' Angelika was awed by him.

'There has been the odd dalliance, but nothing that worked out,' he said with a touch of embarrassment.

'And to think, within six months of running away, I was with the Salvation Army, and far away from Portsmouth, my life totally changed. But I never looked back. We had all gone our separate ways, I've never met another person from school since.' Angelika was sad for a moment for the missed years, she sighed. 'But maybe as we were, it wouldn't have worked out then, anyway.'

'That's all past now. Let's forget the regret and build on those good times, and what we've built together now.' He gave her a reassuring hug.

She nodded, and they talked of friends long forgotten and things they had done and the other hadn't known or didn't remember.

Having come from a stable, loving family, Glen looked shocked when Angelika suddenly blurted out, 'what about my new family I'm just getting to know?'

'Am I not part of it?'

Angelika was horrified at what she'd said, 'Heavens, I never meant it like that. Of course you are. I'm new to all this, please bear with me while I grow up a bit.' A couple of confused tears ran down her face and she rubbed them away with her sleeve.

Nevertheless, she then jumped in with both feet. 'There is one more thing we need to talk about.' She wanted to get everything straight and sniffed some more tears away. 'I trained as a pastor and have worked all my life in some sort of Christian based job. It's part of me, non-negotiable.'

'Why should that be a problem?' He sounded puzzled.

'I believe in a God who created man and woman, who gives us unconditional love, and wants to live in a relationship with us.'

'So why is that a problem, you're not a nun?'

'You've never said what you believe in. You might be an atheist for all I know. We've dodged talking about this.'

'I was brought up in an Anglican family, was confirmed at eleven and have held on to that, even if it wasn't the be all and end all of my life like yours. Is that enough to begin with?' Glen almost pleaded.

'You never said a word about that to me.' Angelika began weeping, although this time in relief that she'd finally found out.

'There are lots of words I want to say to you, and I'm going to spend my life saying them. Will that do?' he said in a firmer voice and pulled her to look at him.

'Glen, is that a proposal?' Angelika's eyes opened in astonishment.

'I'm not doing the bended knee bit, but yes.'

'I'm not sure if I can marry you, Glen.'

He blanched.

'I'm saying yes to Harry and Glen. I want that special feeling and fun we had then, and all that we have now. Can we do both?'

With that, he shoved her over and kissed her like she'd wanted someone to do all her life.

THE FUNERAL

The land swiftly recovered its greenness as the earth under Hamlet absorbed the salt from the days it had been marshes. Things moved on with healing the people, too.

Their first job was repairing the church and graveyard. Terry sorted out the bones, and they all agreed that they would bury Veronica together with her daughter. They didn't use full coffins, but stoutly made boxes lined with lead because of the high groundwater level.

Henry spent hours lovingly creating them in oak and Teresa fitted silken linings. They were to go in holes deeply dug so that if ever a storm came again, they would rest. Proper gravestones with dates and names were ordered and delivered. No family was found for Gerard, so this would remain his home, too.

The church was spring cleaned and Angelika prepared to take the brief committal service in a full vicar's outfit, as Dulcie called it. Angelika also had to go to the local parish church to ask if they could borrow some green matting and lowering straps.

In the vestry, she met a harassed looking vicar, who, as she started giving the story, waved his hands in the air.

'Quite honestly, I'm not interested in a load of old bones washed up in the storm. Do what you like, but bring the straps back by Thursday, as that's my next funeral. I have so many things to do that I can't be involved. The Bishop is coming today for the confirmation service and I haven't even printed the order of service.'

He was gone in a flurry of black and exasperation. Angelika found what she needed and looked around the busy graveyard, which was filled with graves bedecked with flowers and plastic monuments. For the first time ever, she was thankful that her days of running a flock were over.

The day of the internment was dull and sombre in line with their moods. Honey and Poppy even brought the children dressed in dark clothes. Angelika would have liked it to be a colourful celebration of life, but they had all wanted to be sombre, possibly as a form of contrition. Heather and Terry came in late and sat at the back.

Dulcie had raided Teresa's garden, which had missed the flooding in places, as her own garden was lost under scaffolding and debris. She and Teresa used glorious clay pots, so there were at least the bright reds and browns of the winter countryside. Dulcie would have a new garden at Phil and Mary's house in the spring, and Teresa was going to help her. Beau house was now being repaired under the vigilant eye of Terry in case heirlooms were found or damaged. It was going to be a holiday home or Christian retreat centre depending on whether you talked to Angelika or the others.

To begin, everyone sang familiar songs such as Morning has Broken and the Old Rugged Cross, then they sat down, squashed in the pews. Angelika had made it clear she would talk about Veronica, and it was important. As everyone looked at her expectantly, Angelika pulled at the tight dog collar, then sensed a coming of Holy Spirit. Now he was here, she realised how much she had missed him. Yet, this was new, a different, warmer, filling glow. She wanted to sit and bask in him, but they were waiting. Rising to her feet, looked at them with what she hoped was a warm, loving smile.

'We're here to remember Veronica, her daughter, little Dulcie and Gerard. No secret is too dark for God and all that has passed is firmly in his hands. Each one of you can know and will know his forgiveness for things that have happened in times that were so different to now.'

'We know where Veronica is now, but not what she was thinking at the time, as she was ill when she passed away. From what Terry has told us about the family, she was brought up in a Christian home and had been confirmed. Our salvation is safe, once we have accepted Jesus, whatever we go through, his blood on the Cross is sufficient. Veronica is with our heavenly father. Little Dulcie didn't know life, but we can be sure she is also with her father in heaven. Gerard, who passed away as a full and loving member of the living church, is with them there.'

'Let this lift a weight from you as we begin a new phase here in Hamlet. It's not about the money, but God has certainly supplied more of your needs than can be imagined to heal this community. Look at all the coincidences (which you all know I call God incidences) that brought things to a head here.'

'I'm not saying God made the storm, although he may correct me on this, but he used it to bring healing to you all. In the coming months, please just think and reflect on that love is just waiting there for you, no conditions, perfect love. Use Gerard's money wisely to heal, as I'm sure he would have done. Whatever means he used to gain it, turn it now to good.'

'In the coming weeks, pause and meditate on your memories of Veronica and her baby. Turn the blessings outwards that have come to you because of her and share them with others. Let God's healing and forgiveness fill your lives and replace all the bitterness of the past. Now let's say the Lord's prayer together, sing Amazing Grace and lay our friends to rest.'

Dulcie began the song, and not a few people listened in surprise at her strong, vibrant voice. Then the men lifted the two boxes from the front and slowly marched out to the graveyard. A gentle breeze blew around them and as Angelika went through the formal committal ceremony, it sounded to her like a woman's gentle sigh.

Dulcie was in tears as she dropped some flowers on to the boxes and all heard her say, 'Good bye, my little sister.'

AFTERWARDS

Then, of course, they all marched to the café, and further toasts were made. Angelika had gifts for all in the form of one of the gospels, and she took care to say that she hoped the new community would use these to begin afresh. No one made any reactions, but they took them, even the kids with the children's version. Seeds had been sown. There was such a different atmosphere to many of the recent meetings that Angelika really hoped it was the beginning of healing.

Angelika still felt the spirit with her. This was a fresh outpouring for her new life, and she inwardly rejoiced. She chatted to everyone and caught up on their news. Henry's bees were thriving in their new hive, and he had finished his house. Fiona and Mark had re-dug and put new soil on their market garden and were confident of the next year, as was Teresa who was busily re-designing her garden with a pond. Ron and Pete had bought buffaloes, hoping to exploit fresh markets, as were their wives with new breeds of poultry. Both wives had new cars at last! May and Ted were just happy to grow their business.

Gerard's bounty had paid for all of this, and the remainder would be divided up once Steven had got the legality of the estate sorted out. One evening, Angelika and Phil had a heated discussion about his money. It wasn't as if it was his anymore, nor did he need it, but he couldn't let go. Finally, after Angelika stopped the discussion and prayed loudly about it, he actually shut up for a while.

'50/50?' came his best offering the next day, even if it was muttered and he looked away from her. A good family compromise. Angelika promptly put all of the money into the commune funds as she had said she would, to their appreciation and Phil's badly hidden annoyance. Mary laughed at him, which didn't help, but eventually he saw the funny side and let the subject go. Angelika had already asked Steven to put the house into Phil and Mary's new names.

Angelika and Glen found themselves sitting with Heather, who had kept a very low profile throughout the whole ceremony. After thanking Angelika for all she had done for Dulcie, she finally apologised for running away.

'After all those years, the idea of being free of my daughter and Hamlet was too much for me. Believe me, I do love her, but I've been with her since I was about sixteen. I felt there was never any time I could call my own since then. On that day, I walked the streets back to where I grew up, and of course, it was all long gone.'

'The boozer was still there, and inside I found one of my cousins, who told me all about my family. All my parents and brothers are gone. I didn't want to look up nephews and nieces, so I said my goodbyes and walked out. Terry had given me his number, so eventually I rang him and asked if he knew of a cheap hotel. He picked me up after his shift, we went for a meal and talked and talked. I've never really communicated with a man, even at my age! The rest, you know.'

'At last I can use my degree and it is fascinating. Before you ask, this is a friendship, Terry is gay. We work well together. He has found me a small flat, and a job as a cleaner in the hospital. I will be self sufficient. I'm glad Dulcie doesn't want to come back permanently, our relationship was unhealthy at times. She needs to find her own life, as in this today's society she can. She's quite old for Down's so I hope she gets the most of it.'

Angelika winced inwardly at that remark, but what could she do, except wish Heather well? During the service, it had been clear the two women had been ignoring each other. Best leave them a while to sort themselves out. Glen, who was openly eavesdropping on the conversation, saw Angelika's dismay and took her hand. At last, the evening came to a decorous end, and Angelika was relieved to cross the road back to the house, with Dulcie charging ahead to see Stew.

DULCIE MOVES ON

The next day, Heather took all she needed from Beau house and moved to London. There were jokes about the age difference between her and Terry and just what they were working on, but they didn't dare do it in front of Dulcie after Angelika had caught them all gossiping about it in the café.

Dulcie had decided that for now, as she was finally allowed to be an adult, and could choose, she would stay in Hamlet with Phil, Mary and Angelika. She announced it to everyone she met, remaining completely unmoved that her mother had gone, so it was a right decision. Glen went away again for a few days before Christmas, some secret things to do, he said, and Angelika had to be happy with that.

The time came for Dulcie to be rid of her cast, so it was with glee they took off for Bridmouth Hospital. She had already been to the local doctor to be registered. Terry, in his kindness, had arranged everything for Dulcie from London, including the vaccinations she had missed. Angelika was bowled over that he had done this.

However, much to Dulcie's fury, over several visits, she was given the various vaccinations that she'd never had. She yelled and screamed and then not noticed the needle being slipped in by a nurse who knew all the tricks in the book.

Her arm was another thing, she couldn't wait to get rid of the itchy plaster. When her arm emerged, it looked pale and wasted, and so she was booked in with a physiotherapist to get it back to normal. He came to book Dulcie's appointments and show her some exercises. It was all Angelika could do not to laugh as Dulcie went all coy again. Well, at least she would be keen to be there for her appointments and do the exercises.

If Dulcie was really going to be a woman, then there were some things to do. Outside the hospital, Angelika turned to her.

'Dulcie, when did you last have your hair cut?'

'Don't know.' She was suddenly mulish.

'Did your mother do it?'

She nodded and looked down.

'So how would you like to go to a proper hairdresser, with mirrors and capes and lots of products to try?'

Dulcie lit up, so they trotted off to the same hairdresser who had sorted Angelika's dreadlocks out all those months ago. Dulcie glowed as she was seated and gowned, she smiled at herself in the mirror.

'How short would you like it?' asked the hairdresser.

'NOT SHORT,' she shouted. 'I want it long, like a princess. I enjoy flicking it, it's never been so long.' The mulish look returned.

He was more than a match for her. 'Then how about I just even it up at the ends, so it's all neat?' He had said the right thing as she nodded.

'Would you like to have it all the same colour, possibly some highlights?' That brought a huge grin back to her face. He fetched a catalogue and together they chose the colours. Angelika was right, the man was a genius. Two hours later, Dulcie looked ten years younger and knew it, she couldn't keep away from the mirrors as Angelika settled up.

They weren't finished yet. Next came a large department store with an extensive makeup department. For a moment, while Dulcie looked at the mirror again, Angelika caught the eye of an assistant who was made up as if she were getting ready for a big do, not simply work. She explained what she wanted, and Dulcie wandered over.

For a split second, Angelika froze, was the woman going to make some comment or refuse? But no, she studied Dulcie's face, then gestured to a chair and Dulcie was once again bedecked.

'You have amazing skin, so we don't need to use much foundation or powder. Your blue eyes will make it easy to bring out the best.'

Dulcie was totally silent as the woman deftly applied light makeup and highlighters, not using mascara, as she must have realised Dulcie might have problems with the finer skills needed for that. She gave Dulcie a simple look that made her more alive and colourful. It was a complete transformation from the sad woman who Angelika had first met.

She slept less too. Sitting on a chair to watch the process, Angelika wondered if Heather had encouraged her to nap to give her some peace. Dulcie had lost weight, going for daily walks with Stew and Angelika, not sitting in front of the TV all day. Even so, she had found Mary enjoyed the same soaps, and the two were often found snuggled up on the settee with snacks, enjoying the shows and company, even if sometimes Mary couldn't explain what was going on to Dulcie's satisfaction.

Dulcie was then shown how to do the makeup herself and given samples of cleansers, toners, and all sorts of wonderful things. She left the shop with a huge bag and looking happier than ever in her life. She didn't want earrings, which had been Angelika's other idea, so they went to the electrical department.

Here, Dulcie had her first phone and a CD player for home. The look on her face when she heard the music in her head for the first time made Angelika burst out laughing, and Dulcie joined in with joy. Another bill was paid, but Angelika didn't care, Phil had given her his credit card.

He was finding having two daughters a challenge, never having had any children to bring up. More than once, Mary and Angelika had to explain to him the things Dulcie couldn't understand nor do. With Angelika he was happier, showing her the hidden photos of his life and telling her x rated stories, forgetting her convictions and beliefs. Mary, the ever motherly figure, smoothed over any difficult situations and comforted Angelika, telling her it was all pretty much normal family life. In many ways, she was as new to it all as Dulcie.

ANGELIKA MOVES ON TOO

It was during this time before Christmas that Angelika knew that God was calling her attention to things she needed to deal with in her life. Finding the new world of family was almost like a re-birth, but at the same time, she knew she was lacking somewhere, that she was deficient, she was carrying wounds, and these she mustn't carry into her married life.

She took to having early morning walks along the beach, even though it was bitterly cold at times. She prayed and talked, but was unable to discern what he was telling her. Stew faithfully came along, faithfully sitting beside her by the breakwaters as if she knew what it was and wished she could tell her.

One day in late December, Angelica and Mary took Dulcie to a day centre in Bridmouth, where she met many others like herself. They watched from the door as she marched in and found people like her who understood her and were on the same wavelength. Dulcie was deliberately placed at a craft table with two other Down's syndrome ladies, who at first took issue at her staring at them.

Then Dulcie grinned at them, 'I'm like you, we're beautiful princesses!' That broke the ice, and the three spent the morning crafting, talking, and laughing together, and the ladies told Dulcie about how they were different with a great deal of pride. Dulcie grew in that day, and asked Angelika even more questions about life, some of which she did not know how to answer.

After a couple of sessions, Dulcie insisted Angelika and Mary go away, they were being boring, but they also suspected it was something to do with Geoff who was her new best friend. Dulcie was growing up.

It was the next morning, on what Angelika was now calling her walk and wrestle with Jesus, that things finally fell into place. In her mind, she saw the look on Dulcie's face when she saw Geoff at the centre and wanted Angelika gone. Her feelings were a stab of pure jealousy. That horrified and sickened her at the same time. She knew she loved her sister, but to think like that?

Then again, she had never been so close to a family member in her entire life, was Angelika still a child too? It wasn't as if she didn't have Glen, and she knew that was love, too. Phil annoyed her like mad at times, and she resented the years they had missed together, and she didn't mind that he had Mary. What was this all about?

To her mind came Corinthians 13, and as she read it on her phone, the words rang out in her head; the meaning was trying to leap out of the page to her. She prayed in tongues and waited for the translation.

Finally. Love has nothing to do with loving a sister, a father or a husband. It is love; it has the same qualities whoever we are. Nothing to do with gender. She was jealous of Dulcie because she looked like loving someone else, and Angelika hadn't been mature in loving to understand and had such skewed ideas that they clouded the truth. Love is unconditional.

It didn't mean that Dulcie was in some weird way being unfaithful. Angelika had the same love for Phil, and knew she was polluting it with something else, and she sensed Jesus would give that to her in a minute. She loved Glen, and that was the sexual love for a man, but deeper, deeper down, after all their platonic past they had, she saw it was for him, a companion, her earthly buddy, her soul mate, as much as she hated that expression when others used it.

The thing that tainted it was when sex or lust got in the way, and from her misspent youth, she had allowed herself to mistake that for love. Now she felt the difference like a blade going through her. Like a washing of the spirit, she got what those hippies had been trying to spread all over the world. She said sorry to God for all her bad and wrong thoughts and feelings in the past. Love was the strongest thing in the world, but it was so easily tainted when the truth of it isn't seen.

So what was up with her and Phil? She wanted this cleared, sorted, newly washed before the wedding. Shivering, she sat and prayed on, eyes clamped shut. Tell me.

Honour Your Father and Mother.

It was about forgiveness. We all blunder, and her parents certainly had. She became aware of the deeply buried resentment she had for Phil and her mother. First, she had to honour them as parents, despite all the mess they had made of theirs lives and hers. They were her very own damaged folks who had, in turn damaged her. Letting go of her anger led to forgiveness, recognition, and understanding. As she acknowledged her parents, a weight deep inside her lifted.

Tears flowed and belly deep groans released the pain that had been holding her down all her life. Soon, smiling and crying, she made her way home, glad the rain was now washing the tears away, and Stew was leaping and bounding in recognition of the healing.

WEDDING

Dulcie and Angelika had enjoyed their first family Christmas with all the trimmings and were already looking forward to the next as they took the decorations down. Glen was far more used to such things and had often laughed at and with the pair in their excitement, especially on Christmas morning.

Dulcie had been cross when Angelika told her she was getting married in a registry office. She had talked so much of the princess dress she wanted for it. They gently explained to her that the real, God part of the wedding would take place in the church in Hamlet, this was just for all the form filling. She then understood that Angelika couldn't take the service herself and anyone might say some words to celebrate a wedding in a place registered for it, and this would be in their church.

Early in the new year, they made the registry office ceremony with little fuss. The bride and groom wore jeans, still much to Dulcie's annoyance. She cheered up, however, when Brian and Sue came down to have a winter holiday to run some services and meetings while they stayed with May and Ted.

Angelika had felt it best for her to step back from the growing faith in the community, as she was too close to them. She wanted them to find their way without the pressure of her being there. It wasn't as if they were all now fervent, Bible reading church goers, but there was an air of friendship and tolerance that hadn't been there before. There were fewer arguments and more helping out. Perhaps this community that was breaking out of its shell was becoming what had been dreamed of in the drug riddled mind of Veronica.

On the day, dressed in her simple white frock, Angelika looked out of her bedroom window down to the sea. She now knew the fulness of God's love and finally understood why she had felt her anointing as a pastor leave her. She was at peace with herself, no longer wanting to minister after years of serving all over the world.

Angelika would now be half of a pair, maybe even a mother. God had given her a family beyond anyone's craziest dreams. He had used her to bring healing to Hamlet, using so many coincidences to bring things into play. She had been more of a real pastor in the past few months than in the rest of her life.

That such love could come to her was his complete blessing. The mature love of a woman for a man was an alien world for her, she had no guidelines from childhood to follow. She was also determined that her memories of teenage lust would not taint this adult love. It would mean learning to share and compromise, and she ached with the relief of never having to be on her own again.

Her only pain was for her mother, who was so lost, and nothing could be done. But now, at last, she could love her parents and forgive the faults. Angelika could only hope that when she had asked the Salvation Army to keep an eye on her mother that they had really helped her before her too early death. Enough. Today was the only day in her life which would be so special, and she so wanted her there, but it would never be.

Before Angelika walked with Phil to the car, she went to visit her ducks. She walked carefully so as not to get her dress mucky. The ducks were dabbling away in a corner, but swam over to see her, now being used to people feeding them treats all the time.

The ducklings now had their full set of feathers and were smaller versions of their parents. Phil had said several times he fancied roast duckling, and even Stew had growled at him in the uproar. The duck and drake looked up at her, as if taking in that she was the same colour as them, quacked loudly, then swam majestically back to eat, not disgusted at no bread, but in a ducky approval. Stew stood at Angelika's side.

'My little friend, I'll be back soon, look after Dulcie?' Stew put her head on one side and Angelika could have sworn she understood. Together, they walked back into the house.

When Angelika and Phil arrived at the church, it was lit with candles and filled with greenery that had been harvested from the hedgerows. Henry was to run the service, as he said to anyone who would listen that as the eldest in Hamlet, it was his job.

Amazing Grace was played on a loud CD player as the bride came in on the arms of her father, who was so proud he wanted to burst. She caught Glen's eye and had to turn away from not laughing in joy as he turned to her with a huge grin.

The celebration words, thanking God for all the coincidences that had brought change and healing to the community, then committing Angelika and Glen into their new lives together, were read by Dulcie in the sparkliest frock that could be found. Everyone heard her soft voice, and there were tears in many eyes.

Phil read Angelika's now favourite Bible reading from Corinthians 13, and then they sang Shine, Jesus, Shine, the song that Angelika and Dulcie had first sung together. Everyone belted that out, as Dulcie had reminded them to learn it every time she saw someone.

Then came the wedding march, and outside, the happy couple was covered in confetti. There were no council or church rules here to stop it from being chucked at will.

The party took place, of course, at the café which was now refurbished for new guests in the spring as they didn't need to keep Hamlet secret and discourage visitors anymore. The cake was, of course, enormous and, naturally, made by May. Fiona and Mark had supplied a ham, Honey and Poppy the eggs for sandwiches and cakes.

Steven Stephens had been invited and used the speeches to make an announcement that had them all raising their glasses for a toast. He and Angelika had been in touch as he was still trying to get a birth certificate for Dulcie as Terry had done all he could do. It was taking time and although not a problem practically, as there might never be a need for it. Angelika liked things tied up and sorted.

'I've known for a while, but have been saving this for a special occasion.' Several drunken boos echoed this. When they quietened, he continued. 'I have been in consultation with the Crown estate, and I even had a letter from the King. Terry has written a brief history of Hamlet, which I sent to him, which is why he got so involved. The King demands.' More, louder boos.

'The King demands that all the back rent for Hamlet be paid owing to his historical namesake and that it is now paid annually. That you will keep this piece of his land in a way that will please a landlord who is keen on preserving the countryside and environment. I have the bill here, so you better have a whip round. It's £252!' There was a huge cheer with notes and coins thrown at him, which he skilfully ducked.

Like the ending of Dicken's Scrooge, all had come good and would be in the future. There was no discord, it was a perfect party to be remembered for years to come. Glen danced with his new sister in law, who trod on his feet and laughed. Phil spun his daughter off her feet, and Henry was seen hand jiving at his table with a large glass of wine at his side.

Angelika and Glen were picked up by a brand new Land Rover because no limousine would come down the track. The bouquet was thrown and caught by Dulcie, who, when Phil explained to her what it was for, went bright red and gave it to Honey's daughter.

The couple were being whisked off somewhere hot and sunny, then a trip to the states. Glen promised that these trips and dashing offs would end, as he was finalising the management for his new business in the US. Angelika didn't mind what they did as she was still in love with being a family member and had to be reminded that they would still all be there when they returned. Whatever this new life would involve, where ever she and Glen went, she would be part of a family.

As the Land Rover chugged away, Phil looked

at Henry and Roy. 'Now, as soon as you move in with Roy, Henry, I think we should have a look at your house if we're to have it ready for the happy couple when they return. I've got some brilliant ideas...'

DEAR READER, THANK YOU!

I hope you have enjoyed Legacy. My other Christian novel, Tom is also available on Amazon.

Please leave a review on Amazon.It means so much to indie authors!

There are many ways to catch up with my books. My blog, Anna's Horse Books, on the Homepage, just click on follow by email at the foot of the page, or click on the follow widget if you are on Wordpress.

https://booksbyanna619772285.wordpress.com/

You can also join me in my Facebook group for horse book readers. Horse Books for Grown Ups.

https://
www.facebook.comgroups/1979909005465261

My Author page on Facebook

https://www.facebook.com/horsesandogs

Printed in Great Britain
by Amazon

31867161R00142